GW00836014

The Truth Will Out

BRIAN CLEARY

Aisling,

Hope you enjoy it!

Best wishes in the future.

Brian

Copyright ©Brian Cleary 2016

The Truth Will Out

By Brian Cleary

ISBN-13: 978-1537645391

ISBN-10: 1537645390

ALL RIGHTS RESERVED

The right of Brian Cleary to be identified as the Author of this book has been asserted by Brian Cleary.

No part of this publication may be reproduced, stored in or introduced into a retrieval system, or transmitted, in any form or by any means (electronic, mechanical, photocopying, recording or otherwise) without the prior written permission of the author.

This author is from Ireland and writes using Irish spellings and dialect.

Rogena Mitchell-Jones, Literary Editor
RMJ Manuscript Service LLC
www.rogenamitchell.com

To Mam

Chapter 1

Midlands Prison
Ireland
15th May 2012

"THE TRUTH WILL out. The truth will out. The truth will out." He kept repeating his late father's old saying as he walked slowly towards the visiting room.

For over forty years, he had been waiting for this day.

Today was the day that the truth would finally free him.

He had faced many trials and tribulations in his life, but now as he entered the Visitors Room, he had never felt more nervous. He had always known this day would come. It was the thought of this day that had kept his mind going for all those years. While those closest to him and those who had campaigned for justice had given up, he never had. He had always prayed that one day he would be set free.

He received the urgent phone call late the previous night. Tom Dylan, his long-suffering solicitor, had called to say that he needed to see him—the matter was of the utmost importance. He had just received new information that struck at the very core of his case.

"Will it set me free?" he asked.

After a long pause, Tom answered, "Yes, it should. I'm not going to discuss this any further over the phone, however. I'll be up to see you first thing in the morning."

"What do you mean by 'should'? Tom, you need to tell me. Will it set me free?" he repeated slowly.

There was silence at the other end of the phone. He was just about to repeat his question when Tom answered, "Yes, it will set you free. I'll see you in the morning."

He was just about to ask what new information had come up after all these years when he heard the phone go dead.

Apparently, he had not slept that night as he tossed and turned, replaying the phone conversation over and over in his mind. What new information could there be? It had all happened so long ago. The case had captured the imagination of a nation and had dominated front pages.

Even now, on each anniversary of that horrendous night, it would leap back into the media spotlight again. There had been numerous documentaries made about that night, and Hollywood had even made a movie. He remembered how that 'Yank' director had constantly plagued him to co-operate with the making of the film and to 'tell his side of the story.' Yankee had even promised him money, over a million dollars, if he would talk.

"Look, Buddy, you can use it when you get out," he said.

"Get out," he had said to himself at the time. If only he knew. He chuckled when he remembered what he said to the fancy American, who had tried to sweet talk him on numerous occasions.

"To quote a line from a great man and a great film, *The Field*— 'Go home, Yank,'" he said to him all those years back, and then he turned on his heel and walked away.

The film had been a great success and went on to win an Oscar—best male actor. He had never seen it or had an interest or intention of ever seeing it. He had heard recently that the 'Yank' was thinking of a re-make. *Honestly. Some people!*

Tom was looking good, he thought as he entered the Visitors Room. The years had been kind to him, and the grey hair suited him.

"Hi, it's great to see—"

"I'm sorry, Tom. I don't mean to be rude, but can you please dispense with the small talk?" he interrupted. "You said you had news that will free me."

"Yes, but I think you need to sit down. This is going to come as a major shock to you and—"

"Please Tom, just get on with it," he interrupted again, but this time, he couldn't hide the aggression in his voice.

"Sure, sure. I'm sorry. It's just that, anyway... Does the name Professor Hamilton mean anything to you?"

"Who?"

"Professor Hamilton?" repeated Tom.

"No. Definitely never heard of him. What's he a professor of?

"Endocrinology."

"I knew it. I knew it. Didn't I always say, Tom, that the advances in forensic science and DNA would solve this case? Thank God this day has finally arrived."

"Now, don't be getting ahead of yourself—1971 was a very long time ago. The guards still haven't been able to locate the file. As far as I know, they haven't even bothered to look for it in the last eight years. Even if they manage to find the file, there is no guarantee whatsoever that the semen found on Mary Kate will be there. Remember, in 1971, there was no such thing as DNA evidence. It wasn't even on the horizon. Why would they bother to keep a semen sample? At that stage, fingerprinting was as good as it got."

He tried to interrupt him, but Tom continued. "And, if by some miracle, the semen is there, what condition do you think it would be in? Do you really believe they will be able to learn anything from a forty-year-old sample? I'm sorry, it's just not

3

possible."

The two men looked at each other in silence for a long moment.

"So he isn't forensics. What is he then?"

"Was he. Do you remember, during the trial, I told you that I received a number of anonymous letters telling me they had the wrong man?"

"Yes, I remember."

"Well, he wrote those letters."

Chapter 2

JAMIE WATCHED MARY KATE striding purposefully towards the front door as he peeped out from behind his bedroom curtain. The shit was going to hit the fan—she was definitely going to tell. Mam would be upset and worse, disappointed in him. However, it would be nothing compared to how his father would react when he came home. He'd kill him this time for sure. And he had only promised him the other day there would be no more incidents—fuck it anyway.

Jamie hadn't meant to lose his temper, but then again, he never did. After his latest promise, he had been trying very hard to suppress the anger that would build up inside of him. At twelve years of age, he was starting to recognise the early warning signs and was learning how to diffuse the 'bomb' that could potentially explode inside his brain. His father had nicknamed his temper 'the bomb'—an apt description considering the mayhem that followed the explosion. It was always violent and impossible to control—Jamie felt overpowered by it. It was as if he were driven by demons, and it left him emotionally and physically drained.

The day couldn't have started any better. Unusually, for a summer's day in Ireland, it was warm and humid. Jamie had finished playing a tennis match earlier and was now involved in a soccer game. The game was close and delicately balanced. Jamie was one of the younger boys playing and was rather quite pleased with his performance. His older brother John had actually even praised him during the game.

The kids were under time pressure—Vincent's mother had already been out once to call him in for lunch. Damien threaded a beautiful pass through to him. Jamie had never scored the winning goal playing with the older boys. He composed himself and was just about to pull the trigger when, WHAM, his legs were taken from underneath him.

"Penalty," he growled as he jumped to his feet turning to see who the hatchet man was.

Shane, Mary Kate's fourteen-year-old cousin, who happened to be visiting for the day, stood facing him.

"No way. I got the ball first. You dived, you cheat."

"I thought it looked like a penalty," Vincent joined in.

"No way," Shane said again, not conceding an inch. "I definitely got the ball. The little prick dived. That's the truth!" exclaimed Shane.

"VINCENT, get in for your lunch right now. Do you think I've nothing better to do than spend my whole life running after you?" Vincent's mother roared.

You didn't cross Vincent's mother. It was decided, in the interest of self-preservation, to call the game a draw. However, Jamie wasn't finished. His big moment had been stolen.

"That's not true. The truth will out!" Jamie screamed at the bigger boy.

"What the fuck are you on about?" Shane went toe to toe with Jamie and laughed in his face.

Big mistake.

The red mist had started to descend, and Shane's last words put him over the edge. Shane was about four inches taller than Jamie was, but that didn't matter. It never did. With his first punch,

6

he knocked Shane to the ground. Jamie immediately jumped on Shane and delivered a flurry of punches before the older boys intervened and managed to pull him off Shane. Two of them held on to him. They had seen it all before and knew that Jamie would have to be restrained for the next minute or so.

In the distance, Jamie could hear Vincent's mother calling him an 'animal' and followed by, "What is wrong with that boy? He should be locked away. It's not normal."

But, worst of all, Mary Kate had seen the whole thing. She had run over and was now helping her cousin to his feet. She was in tears.

"Jamie Ryan, I am so disappointed in you," she said, and then she looked him straight in the eye. "You make it so hard for anybody to like you and be your friend."

Very unfair, Jamie thought—you'd swear the big oaf had been seriously hurt. After all, he got what he deserved.

THE DOORBELL RANG. Here we go, Jamie said to himself. Time to face the music… again.

"Hi, Aunt Mary. Can Jamie come out to play?"

Awesome. She's not going to tell!! How could he have doubted her? She was his best friend, had probably already forgiven him, and was no longer mad at him—she realised that it was Shane's own fault. What a gem of a friend—most of the other suck-ups would have made a beeline for his door, just dying to get him into trouble. But Mary Kate wasn't like all the others.

'Aunt Mary' was a term of endearment Mary Kate used for Jamie's mother. Both sets of parents were very good friends, living just a few hundred yards apart, and the kids had grown up addressing the others' parents as Aunt and Uncle—it was their parents' way of letting the kids know that these people were different than other friends. They were close.

7

"Coming, Mam," a relieved Jamie called out as he skipped down the stairs.

They walked down the road in silence. Jamie guessed that Mary Kate was expecting an apology. However, the words wouldn't come out of his mouth. Jamie had calmed down and now admitted to himself that there was a possibility he was in the wrong. He may have overreacted. But his stubbornness refused to let him say he was sorry. The silence continued.

Eventually, Jamie picked up the courage to apologise.

"How's Shane? Is he all right? I didn't mean to hit him that hard. But he shouldn't have called me a liar. And it *was* a penalty."

So much for an apology!

"Jamie Ryan, for once in your life, will you *please* take responsibility for your own actions and stop blaming other people? You need to grow up," she said sternly and then, after a brief pause, she continued, "Shane's fine. No thanks to you."

Mary Kate was only six months older than Jamie. She had recently turned thirteen. But she was mature well beyond her years. Normally, if anybody spoke to him like that, he would instinctively curse them out of it.

But Jamie fell silent. Mary Kate had never spoken to him in such a harsh, cold manner. It just wasn't in her nature. Jamie was shocked—no, he wasn't shocked, he was devastated. Her words cut to the core. The tears welled up in his eyes. He had blown it—he had lost his best friend. Sometimes, it felt like she was the only person who fully understood him. However, Jamie Ryan hadn't allowed himself to cry since he was five years old. He refused to give ground—his steely determination returned as he quickly regained his composure. He thought of cursing her out of it, but he couldn't do it.

"But—" Jamie finally uttered.

"No buts Jamie." Mary Kate cut across him. "Anyway, I have the matter sorted once and for all. We will not be discussing this any further. DO YOU UNDERSTAND?"

Jamie contemplated continuing but eventually replied sheepishly, "Yes, I do."

"Good. Actually, let's not bother going to the park. You wanna come play in my back garden?" she asked.

Jamie nodded, and the two of them walked together to her house.

Just as they were about to go through the side gate, Jamie suddenly stopped and turned to her.

"Mary Kate, I'm sorry."

"I know you are, Jamie. I'm sorry, too."

He hadn't intended to apologise, but it just seemed the right thing to do. He realised it wasn't that hard, and it made him feel good about himself as if a load had been lifted. Maybe he would apologise more often! But Jamie was puzzled by her response— why was she sorry too? Probably because of the way she spoke to him earlier. Anyway, Jamie decided not to ask her. The matter was now firmly behind him. Or so he thought.

When they entered the back garden, Patrick and Shane were waiting for him. Patrick was Mary Kate's fifteen-year-old brother. He was kind of a friend of Jamie's in as much as a fifteen-year-old boy can be a friend of a twelve-year-old. Jamie thought Patrick was cool, and Patrick gave Jamie the time of day. Half the time Jamie called to play with Mary Kate, he would end up kicking a soccer ball around with Patrick.

Patrick wasn't particularly tall for his age but was strong and wiry. Normally, he was an easygoing boy, but that shouldn't be mistaken as soft. He knew his own mind and possessed a quiet determination. Jamie could see Patrick was not happy, not happy at all. He hadn't been playing the soccer match earlier, but of course, he had heard what had happened. Jamie had beaten up his young cousin—simple as that.

Jamie looked from Patrick to Shane and was shocked. Shane's left eye was badly swollen, and he had a burst lip. There was dried blood on his neck and on his T-shirt. Jamie felt sorry for what he had done. Well, he didn't feel any sympathy for Shane. Jamie was still the aggrieved party, and Shane had brought it on himself. He felt sorry for himself. Looking at Shane's face, there was no doubt his father would get to hear about this one, and there would be a price to pay. But Jamie also felt a macabre sense of satisfaction—he admired his handiwork.

Jamie turned back towards Mary Kate, but she had taken a few steps backwards. She refused to make eye contact with him, just staring down at her feet.

Jamie was unsure what to say or do. He stepped forward, offering to shake hands with Shane. Shane, smiling, moved forward as if to shake Jamie's outstretched hand, but then, suddenly pulled Jamie towards him.

It was only then that Jamie saw the large stick Shane had concealed behind his back. Before Jamie had time to react, Shane swung the stick viciously and struck Jamie solidly on the right side of his head.

Jamie attempted to throw a punch, but he felt his legs go weak. He crumpled in a heap on the ground—he didn't even put out his hands to stop his fall.

Chapter 3

WHEN JAMIE CAME to, he had no idea if he had been unconscious, and if so, for how long. He felt groggy as he slowly struggled to his feet. Mary Kate, Patrick and Shane were playing down at the other end of the garden, swimming in and out of focus. They deliberately ignored him.

"Hi, Jamie. Are you all right there, love?" His 'Aunt' Jane asked, bending over him, concern etched on her face.

Unbeknownst to all the kids, Mary Kate's mother had been watching from the upstairs bedroom window. She was livid earlier when she saw Shane's face and heard Mary Kate's account of what had happened. Her first reaction was to march over to Jamie's house and complain. Shane had been left in her charge for the day, and now, look at the state of his face. But after the initial surge of anger subsided, Jane decided against it. Mary and Dan, Jamie's parents, were close friends, and she knew how upset Mary, in particular, would be. She wouldn't add to their woes.

Jamie's behaviour had been the source of conversation on many a night out together. The child was an enigma. Most of the time, he was a sweet, caring child, but if the switch flicked, within seconds, he could turn into a wild, demented animal, lashing out violently at anything and anybody. There was no rhyme or reason to it. She had seen it herself on occasion. In her opinion, and also in the opinion of her husband, what the child needed was professional help. Jane was actually wary of Jamie and often wondered what would happen when he became an adult—he would then have strength to go with that extraordinary temper.

As Jane watched the events unfolding in her back garden, she decided to let the kids sort it out themselves. In fact, she thought it was a good idea for Jamie to get a taste of his own medicine. Jane figured Patrick and maybe Shane, were going to give Jamie a few clouts but was horrified when she saw Shane strike him with a stick. Her face froze when she realised that Jamie was knocked unconscious, and she ran to his aid immediately.

"Yes. I'm fine!" Jamie replied forcefully. He glanced in the direction of the other kids again, but they continued to ignore him. "I'm going home now," he muttered as he pushed past her.

"Okay, love. See you later then," Jane replied kindly. "Tell your mum I'll call over to see her in a while."

Jamie snuck up to his bedroom and lay on his bed. He was confused and had a splitting headache.

What had just happened?

Had Shane hit him with a stick?

Had he passed out?

The one thing he did know for sure was that Mary Kate had deliberately betrayed him. She had lured him into a trap. He now understood what she had meant when she said, "I'm sorry, too." She had willingly been the bait. He could understand where Patrick was coming from, and he should have anticipated Patrick might give him a thumping. But Mary Kate?

And as for Shane? Fuck. That was low. However, the image of Shane's battered and bruised face came back to him, and he had to admit that Shane had every right to seek vengeance. But to do it in such a cowardly way? Especially when Jamie was offering to make the peace and shake hands? That was the lowest of the low.

As anyone who knew Jamie would have anticipated, Jamie wouldn't take this lying down. He began to plot his revenge. The football pitch had always presented him with opportunities for retribution. He would exact his revenge on Shane and Patrick under the guise of a careless tackle. He'd do it when his older brothers were playing—there would be no retaliation then.

But what would he do to Mary Kate? What could he do? Of all the things that passed through his mind, nothing seemed quite right. They were all too brutal.

Jamie woke up with a start. He must have fallen asleep. His mother was shaking him and rubbing his head.

"Jamie love, wake up. Wake up. Are you all right, darling?" she asked tenderly.

She was trying to remain calm and conceal the anxiety in her voice. Jane had followed Jamie home and filled Mary in on all the days' proceedings. She was at first shocked and upset hearing how Jamie had lost his temper yet again and had beaten up Shane. But those feelings turned to anger when she was then informed of the manner of the retribution—her son had been ambushed and knocked out cold.

Mary had wanted to bring Jamie to the hospital, but Jane, a qualified nurse, assured her there was no need—all the medics would do is observe Jamie for the next twenty-four hours, and Mary could do that herself. If he was vomiting or drifting in and out of sleep, then she should bring Jamie to the hospital immediately.

Jane attempted to lighten the moment.

"Kids will be kids. God, they'll be the death of us," she said.

"You never said a truer word," Mary replied forcing a laugh, and the two women embraced before Jane departed. Mary went straight upstairs in search of Jamie and was frightened when she saw him asleep and sprawled across his bed.

"Are you all right?" she asked again.

Jamie looked into his mother's eyes and tried to work out how

13

much she knew. He figured correctly that it was a loaded question. However, he had already decided he wouldn't tell anybody what had happened earlier—how Mary Kate had betrayed him.

"I'm fine, Mam. I was just a bit tired, so I decided to lie down. I must have fallen asleep. What's up?" Jamie replied.

"Are you sure you're all right, son? Is there anything you want to tell me or to talk about?" Mary asked.

"Nope. Just that I love you." And with that, Jamie jumped up from the bed and gave his mother a big hug and a kiss, following up with one of his big cheeky smiles, the smile he knew always worked on her.

"I'm starving. What's for lunch?" Jamie asked.

Mary studied him carefully and decided she wouldn't force the issue and take him to hospital. He appeared lucid and in good form. She was also fully aware that the morning's altercations would have taken their toll on him emotionally. She knew how close Jamie was to Mary Kate and, to a lesser extent, Patrick. She could see that he was deliberately changing the subject, but she also knew it was futile to push him. If Jamie did not want to talk about something, no amount of prising or persuasion would make him change his mind.

From an early age, Jamie wouldn't share his feelings. He would refuse any offer of help or consolation, and instead, simply clam up and deal with things by himself, in his own way. The only person that Jamie seemed to give an inch to was Mary Kate. Mary Kate was very good with Jamie. She had a great understanding of him. One or two words from her could turn him around and defuse a situation that may have been getting out of hand.

Mary informed Jamie that lunch wasn't ready yet and asked if he would like to come down and help her prepare it. He readily agreed, and the two of them went downstairs to the kitchen and started to prepare lunch, Jamie washing the tomatoes and lettuce and Mary cutting slices of home baked ham.

Fifteen minutes later, just as they were about to sit down and

14

eat, Mary Kate and Shane entered the house through the back door. Mary Kate was funny like that. Sometimes, she would arrive in unannounced through the back door, and other times, she would ring the doorbell and wait to be formally invited in. When Mary saw Shane's face for the first time, she was shocked. Mary was about to reprimand Jamie, but she stopped herself just in time. However, Jamie had caught the look of disgust on her face. He was starting to feel ashamed of what he had done, but he also felt anger beginning to boil up inside him again looking at the two of them standing there.

"Aunt Mary, do you mind if I have a word with Jamie in private?" requested Mary Kate in her quiet but authoritative voice. Mary was well used to Mary Kate's ways, yet she still marvelled that she was only thirteen years of age. Such maturity, she thought as she stood up to leave the room.

"I don't want to talk to YOU in private. In fact, I don't want to talk to you. Full stop. Do you *understand*?" Jamie spat out the words.

"Very well. Then what I have to say, I'll say in front of your mother, if that's what you want. Now, do YOU understand?" replied Mary Kate evenly. "It's your choice."

Before Jamie had a chance to reply, Mary walked out of the kitchen, closing the door without saying a word.

"Look, Jamie, I know you're hurting and very upset with us at the moment, but I'm sorry, it had to be done. Shane is going to be moving to a house near us very soon, and I couldn't have an issue between the two of you going forward. The two of you are my best friends, and I want us all to get along. But, Jamie, you cannot go around hurting people like that, and I thought the only lesson you would understand is the one you got. I still want to be your friend, and I love playing with you, but for things to work out, I need you and Shane to get along. Please, Jamie, think about what I'm saying before you reply. I would hate to lose you as a friend."

"So, you're choosing him over me, is that it?" replied Jamie.

BRIAN CLEARY

However, before Mary Kate could answer, Shane stepped forward and offered his hand. He said nothing, but he looked Jamie straight in the eye. It was not a threatening look but a look of reconciliation.

Jamie didn't know what to do. He had never been in this situation before. He was still trying to digest what Mary Kate had said to him and the thought of not having her as a friend when Shane had stepped forward. Jamie looked over at Mary Kate and then back at Shane.

The two boys shook hands.

Chapter 4

STAY CALM. STAY calm. Don't do it. Please, Lord, help me,
Jamie Ryan said to himself. He knew exactly what he wanted to
do. Just one punch. That's all it would take to break his nose. Just
one punch and he knew Damien would shut his big mouth. At
twenty years of age, Jamie still had a vicious temper, though he
had learned over the years to control it. He had developed a deep
religious belief and would often pray to God to help him overcome
his inner demons and suppress his violent urges.

Up until ten minutes ago, they had all been enjoying a good
night at Damien's twenty-first birthday party. Jamie had been
drinking heavily—after eight pints of Guinness, he had switched to
whiskey and was now on his fourth Jameson.

Mary Kate had arrived late to the party and was in high spirits.
She didn't drink alcohol—she had gotten drunk once and had
decided alcohol was not for her. She didn't like the feeling of not
being in control. Besides, Mary Kate was always high on life; she
didn't need any outside substances to enjoy herself. She was now
teasing Jamie about the state he was in and the fact that he was
slurring his words. He was not at all bothered by Mary Kate's
good-natured banter and, as usual, actually quite enjoyed it. It was

only when Damien joined in that Jamie began to get annoyed. At first, Damien's remarks were also friendly and playful, but then they developed a real cutting edge.

"Look at you. The state of you. Jesus, it's amazing that you can even hold a pint, the size of you. A good job you're on the shorts, eh, Titch." Damien teased. But Jamie could tell there was real malice behind his words. At five foot four, Jamie was indeed short of stature. It was the one jibe that could still rile Jamie. His two older brothers were both over six feet tall.

Jamie knew that Mother Nature hadn't intended him to be small, but that would remain his secret. He had sworn to himself years ago he would not let anybody know his secret, especially not Mary Kate and Shane, his two best friends.

"You know what they say, Damien. Excellent goods come in small parcels," interjected Shane.

"The smallest jockeys have the biggest whips," howled Mary Kate as she stood up and then went over and sat on Jamie's knee, kissing him lightly on the cheek. Damien laughed loudly, mainly because he wanted to impress Mary Kate. He patted Jamie on the head and wandered towards the bar.

"Thanks, you guysss," slurred Jamie. "I wasn't going to do anything."

"We know, Jamie. We didn't doubt you," Shane replied as he watched Damien walk away.

Ever since that day in Jamie's kitchen when they shook hands, Jamie and Shane had slowly but surely become the best of friends. Their friendship really blossomed during their school days as they ended up starting secondary school together. St. Joseph's College wasn't the nearest school in the neighbourhood, but it was a young, ambitious school, whose headmaster had greatly impressed Jamie's parents when they attended the school's open day.

However, the biggest deciding factor for them as they chose a school for Jamie was St. Joseph's commitment to sport. Jamie's father felt that rugby, the number one sport at St. Joseph's, would be ideal for Jamie, as it was highly physical but also intensely disciplined. As Shane's parents were new to the neighbourhood, they decided to follow their lead and enrolled Shane there.

When they started in St. Joseph's, neither of the boys knew anyone in their class because no other kids from their area were going to St. Joseph's. Shane was older than Jamie and was in the year ahead of him, but they cycled to and from school together every day. By the time the first Christmas at their new school came, the incidents of the summer were well and truly behind them.

Jamie took to rugby like a duck to water. His father's decision turned out to be one of his best decisions in his life. Jamie absolutely loved the game, and it acted as the ideal channel for all his pent-up aggression. However, Jamie had managed to get himself sent off twice before Christmas in his first year of playing rugby, as he struggled to control his, by now, legendary temper.

The first time was in his second competitive match for the school. Because he was small, Jamie's first match had been for the B-team. He played brilliantly in that first game and was then promoted to the A-team for the next match. Jamie was selected at scrum-half. He was delighted, as that position meant plenty of action. Their coach, Fr. Daly, had warned them not to expect too much and told them to simply enjoy the game.

The match was a local derby against Terenure College, a neighbouring school of St. Joseph's. Terenure College had a distinct advantage over St. Joseph's as their primary feeder school also played rugby. So, when the two teams met in September, the lads from St. Joseph's had only been playing rugby for less than a month, whereas the Terenure pupils had been playing for over seven years. To add to the rivalry that existed between the schools, Terenure was a private, fee-paying school, whereas St. Joseph's was not. The pre-match nerves for the St. Joseph's boys were enormous.

The match went pretty much to form, St. Joseph's showing

more guts and determination, but Terenure College were easy winners due to their superior ball-handling skills. However, wee Jamie Ryan managed to get a consolation try in the last minute of the match. However, as he went over to score his first ever try, the big number six from Terenure fell on him and, in Jamie's mind, deliberately kneed him in the lower back. Jamie jumped up like lightning and threw a flurry of punches at him. He had to be restrained by the referee and was immediately sent off.

His second sending off was a far more serious incident. About four weeks later, in a very tight game against Castleknock, Fr. Daly was barking instructions from the side-line, particularly aimed at Jamie, telling St. Joseph's to keep the game tight and to play ten-man rugby. However, with three minutes to go, Jamie decided to go blindside and attempt a grubber kick to his winger. If it had come off, the winger would have scored a try and the game was theirs. But it was not to be. The opposite winger was alert to the danger. He scooped up Jamie's kick and ran the length of the pitch, scoring what turned out to be the winning try.

As he was running back to his teammates to celebrate the try, he ruffled Jamie's hair and said, "Thanks for the present, you wee prick." Jamie swung a kick at him before he knew what he was doing, catching him just above the knee. The boy went down as if he had been shot. The referee, having seen everything, sent both boys off.

But worse was to come. As Jamie was going off the pitch, Fr. Daly came up to him and berated him for the stupidity of his move and his sending off.

Jamie saw red and told Fr. Daly to, "Fuck off and stick your rugby where the sun don't shine."

Fr. Daly was appalled. He had heard that wee Ryan was a fierce hothead, but this behaviour was totally unacceptable. To cap it all, Jamie's father was there to see his son play for the first time. He immediately intervened and took Jamie away.

A half-hour later, an embarrassed and humiliated Jamie Ryan

shuffled into the dressing room and openly apologised to Fr. Daly and his teammates. He was fortunate that Fr. Daly was a soft man. He said to Jamie that he was forgiven and the matter was in the past, never to be mentioned again.

Then he grabbed Jamie by the jersey, pushed him up against the wall in front of everyone, and said, "But if you ever speak to me or behave like that again, you will never play rugby under my wing as long as I'm in St. Joseph's. Now, go take a shower."

Looking back on it, it was probably the kick in the arse Jamie needed. Jamie was now more determined than ever to be the master of his temper, rather than to be a slave to it. Furthermore, his anger began to impact on Jamie's ability to make friends—the other boys were wary of his outbursts and had started to avoid him. From that day on, he vowed that he would be in total charge of his emotions and that he, and only he, would control his destiny. However, he was to receive significant assistance from a source that he never even considered.

Jamie found God.

Yes, Jamie Ryan found God. He had not set out to find Him. In actual fact, it could be said that He had found Jamie. It happened during the Easter holidays in his first year of school. Like most families in Ireland at the time, Jamie's family was Roman Catholic, and his parents were devout and conscientious. This meant, not only did they go to mass every Sunday, but during Lent, like most of the population, they expected and forced their children to go to Mass every day. Jamie had turned thirteen and found the formalities of Mass utterly and totally boring. He had a deep personal relationship with his God but didn't see the point of Mass. Truth be told, he had decided Mass was counterproductive. Jamie reasoned that all the ritual and the cold Sunday mornings turned people, especially young people, away from religion.

He'd had a heated discussion with his parents before he made his Confirmation the previous year. How was he, at twelve years of age, meant to be in a position to 'confirm' his faith? He wasn't allowed to work, marry, or take a drink, but he was expected to be able to confirm that the Roman Catholic religion was the one and only religion for him. Surely, this very personal decision shouldn't be made en masse, through schools, at such a young age.

His father had listened patiently to all of Jamie's arguments and called his bluff. Eventually, he told Jamie, he agreed with him and would call up to the school the next day and inform his teacher and the priest that Jamie wouldn't be making his confirmation.

"A pity about the confirmation money, though. It would have come in handy for you. But I suppose it's a question of principle," he said as Jamie went to bed that night.

Later on that night, Jamie came back downstairs and explained that he was comfortable with his faith. He would proceed to make his confirmation—he had merely been making the point for others who weren't as sure as him.

"Agreed," said his father with a wry smile.

On that cold Tuesday during the Easter holidays, Mary Ryan hauled Jamie up out of a warm bed and marched him off to ten o'clock mass. There were always special prayers to be said for something or somebody, and today was no exception. Jamie's eldest brother was starting his Leaving Certificate soon, and the customary candles had to be lit. Jamie sat there, bored and brooding as usual, and begun to have a chat with God. It was one of those 'show me a sign' chats that kids regularly have with God.

"Look, Lord, you know I've already started skipping Mass. If you're not happy with that, just show me a sign, and I'll get it sorted," he stated during the Consecration.

Jamie thought nothing more of it and sleepily joined the queue for Communion later on during the mass. He completely froze when, just as the priest was placing the Holy Communion in his hand, he felt a rush of warm air across his palm, and the communion landed on the ground. The priest was unimpressed, bent down, picked up the 'Body of Christ' and went to place it in Jamie's hand again. Once more, there was a rush of warm air across the palm of his hand and the communion landed again on the ground. Jamie knew that he had not dropped the communion and that the wind, The Holy Spirit, was present and showing him a *sign* he had earlier asked for. It was evident by the priest's annoyance that he could not feel this warm wind, and he bent down and retrieved the communion for the second time. But this time, he placed it back in the chalice and gave Jamie a different host that Jamie received into his hand. Jamie returned to his seat in total shock.

That incident copper fastened Jamie's faith, which he soon found to be an indispensable tool in battling his inner demons. Jamie constantly talked to God—not only when he was alone in his room at night, but also throughout the hustle and bustle of the day. Jamie never really asked Him for anything, but these conversations gave Jamie an inner peace that he had not previously enjoyed. Any worries or concerns would simply be placed in God's hands, and any anxiety would simply disappear. At one stage, Jamie even contemplated joining the priesthood, but he knew his heart was not fully committed to it—he didn't agree with the celibacy rules.

The biggest outward change in Jamie was, with God's guidance—which is how Jamie saw it, he learnt how to control his temper. It wasn't an overnight success, but Jamie had managed to stay one step ahead of his temper. However, it was a constant struggle for him, and he had to work hard at it. When the 'bomb' was about to go off, Jamie had developed techniques that would help him to stay calm and rational, and one of the biggest ones was talking to God.

"Thank you, Lord, yet again," Jamie whispered to himself as Mary Kate pulled him towards the dance floor. He hadn't realised how drunk he was until he tried to dance with her. His mind was willing, but his coordination was letting him down badly. Mary Kate was laughing at him and holding him up as he staggered around the floor.

"Keep it steady, Big Boy," Mary Kate teased as he fell against her yet again.

"Yea. Love youuu," he slurred.

"Love you too," she whispered in his ear as she gave him a gentle kiss on the cheek.

At that moment, it finally dawned on him—something he had been missing for all these years. He had never seen Mary Kate in any other light other than as his best friend. How could he have been so stupid? They were made to be together. She loved him, and he loved her. It would be so perfect.

He turned towards her, holding her in a strong embrace, and kissed her forcefully on the lips. However, his kiss didn't get the response he thought it would.

"Jamie, stop it," she whispered to him urgently. "It wouldn't work out."

He looked into her chocolate-brown eyes and was amazed that he hadn't noticed how beautiful she was before now. She had shoulder length brown hair and a flawless complexion. At five foot eight inches, she was slim and perfectly toned. Her breasts, her hips, her shoulders, all were in perfect proportion. She was suddenly revealed to him in all her beauty and grace.

"No. You're wrong. It'll be great. Seriously, we're soul mates. It was meant to be," he said as he then fondled her bottom and hugged her tight to his body. He attempted to kiss her again.

"NO." She pushed him away with all her strength. He fell to the floor.

"What the fuck do you think you're doing, Jamie?" she shouted at him.

"I thought you said you loved me?" he replied.

The music stopped abruptly. A crowd was gathering around them.

"I do love you, Jamie, but not like that. Never like that. Jesus, Jamie. How could you be so stupid?" Mary Kate cried as she turned and ran off the dance floor.

Jamie tried desperately to analyse what had just happened.

24

Had he hurt Mary Kate? Why was she so upset with him? He knew his mind was racing, thoughts flashing in and out, jostling for attention. He tried hard to concentrate and to calm himself. *Lord Jesus, help me in my hour of need*, he prayed, but it didn't ease the commotion in his head. The room was full of eyes, staring and mocking him. Damien was laughing heartily and pointing at him. Jamie had never been so humiliated. He had never thought of Mary Kate as a tease before now, but it dawned on him that it was exactly what she was.

"Mary Kate, that's the last time you'll ever treat me like that," Jamie said in a low growl that even frightened him. He hadn't meant it to sound so menacing. Jamie knew he was on the verge of losing control. Before anybody had time to react, he turned and walked out of the pub.

Please, please, Lord, let me stay calm, he implored as he pushed through the door.

He walked out into the wet night, past a wall of empty Guinness barrels.

"*In actual fact, Lord, stay the fuck out of my way,*" he screamed as he picked one up and hurled it through the plate glass window of the pub. *Fuck the lot of them,* he told himself as he walked away from the explosion of glass.

Damien and two bouncers were about to go after Jamie, but Shane got to the door first. He stood in front of them, barring their way.

"Let him go. I'll sort it," he commanded, looking Damien straight in the eye. At six-foot-four and nineteen stone, Shane was known as a gentle giant, and Damien had never seen him issuing an order. Damien agreed and instructed the bouncers to leave it at that.

Chapter 5

JAMIE RYAN WOKE up with a start. He felt extremely groggy and had a pounding headache. His tongue felt all furry, and he couldn't get his eyes to focus. He was fully clothed and still had his shoes on. He had absolutely no idea where he was.

As his eyes slowly started to focus, he looked around to see if he could recognise anything familiar. The first thing he noticed was the cream carpet that he was lying face down on. Very, very slowly, he turned his head and recognised one of Mary Kate's paintings on the wall. He was on the floor of Mary Kate's apartment, but he had no idea how he got there. He tried hard to remember where he had been the night before. He had had blackouts before because of his drinking, but he had a feeling this one would be particularly bad. He couldn't remember anything about the previous night or how he had ended up here.

Ever since Mary Kate's parents had bought the apartment two years ago, Jamie and Shane, Mary Kate's cousin, were regular visitors. They would often stay the weekend if they were socialising in Dublin city. The three of them were very close and did most things together. The apartment was a two-bed apartment just off Baggot Street within easy walking distance of Dublin city centre. It was part of a small apartment block—just four apartments over two storeys. Mary Kate had given both Jamie and Shane a key, and they tended to come and go as they pleased.

Jamie began the process of piecing together the events of the previous day. Whenever he had blackouts, he would start by trying to remember what had happened the previous morning. He had gone to college as normal and then he remembered he was meeting Shane at The Oak Tavern for a few drinks before going. Where was he going after that? Oh, Jesus. He felt sick to the core of his being as images of Damien's party came flooding back and his attempt to kiss Mary Kate. Not since that childhood incident had there been a cross word between them. He didn't know how she was going to react now, but he knew he had been totally out of order. He would apologise immediately. He then had an image of an empty Guinness barrel being thrown through a window, shards of glass flying in every direction and faces numb with shock staring at him.

Oh, my God. Had he done that?

O Lord, please tell me I didn't do that?

The picture in his head was frightening. He knew that he had totally lost it last night. Would he ever be forgiven?

"I think I have a pulse."

"Are you sure? When will the medics be here?"

Jamie thought he must be dreaming. He hoped he would wake up in his own bed at home. He closed his eyes, counted to ten, and opened them again. He could still feel the cream carpet against his face and could see Mary Kate's painting. But what about the voices? He turned his head slowly, looking in the direction of where the voices were coming from.

The sight that he saw would haunt him for the rest of his life.

Mary Kate lay motionless on the floor. The cream carpet around her head was a dark red colour. She was naked from the waist down, and some buttons on her blouse had been ripped off. One breast was exposed as if it had been manhandled out of the cup of her pink bra.

There appeared to be two men in the room. One was standing over Mary Kate, the other holding Mary Kate's arm. He was checking for a pulse.

He was checking for a pulse?

28

Please, Lord God. Let it not be true. End this nightmare!

Jamie tried to refocus his eyes as he felt the blood drain from his head. He wasn't sure whether he was going to pass out as he began to move his body.

"He's coming to. I'll take him. You stick with the girl. For God's sake, where are the medics?" Jamie heard the man who was standing say. The men were police officers. Just at that moment, the door flew open, and the ambulance crew rushed in.

"I think I have a pulse. I think I have a pulse," shouted one of the guards.

"That's great. Step aside now please," commanded the ambulance driver as he knelt down beside Mary Kate. Within what appeared to be a matter of seconds, Mary Kate was strapped to a stretcher and whisked out of the apartment.

Jamie Ryan lay still on the floor. He now knew that he wasn't dreaming, but he still couldn't believe what was happening in front of his eyes. He prayed to God. He prayed hard.

At first, he didn't pray for Mary Kate, but he prayed that God would help him make sense of the images his eyes were sending to his brain. He still couldn't or he refused to comprehend what was happening. Then he suddenly thought of Mary Kate, her lifeless half-naked body lying in a pool of her own blood. He lifted his head and vomited.

"Are you all right, son?" asked Detective Sergeant Dave Cullen.

Jamie looked up to see the smaller of the two guards standing over him. He tried to speak, but no words would come out of his mouth. His mouth was dry, and his brain just couldn't engage. He groaned. As he did so, the other guard, Detective Inspector Dermot Flood, grabbed him up by his collar and pulled him to his feet.

"You fucking scumbag. What did you do?" Flood screamed straight into his face, his spittle landing all over Jamie. Twisting Jamie's arm around his back, he pulled it up so far that Jamie was sure his arm would snap. Before Jamie knew it, he was in handcuffs.

"Come on, son. You can tell me all about it down at the station," said Detective Sergeant Cullen as he gently prised Jamie away from Flood. Jamie Ryan had never in his short life been in trouble with the law. However, he thought he would be terrified if he had been, but at the moment, he could feel no emotion. All he could think of was Mary Kate. He barely heard what the two guards were saying as he prayed with all his heart that Mary Kate would survive.

Chapter 6

"WHY DID YOU do it?" asked Detective Sergeant Cullen gently.

"I don't know," replied Jamie in a barely audible whisper.

"Was it because she rejected you earlier on at the party? You probably didn't intend to do what you did, but your temper got the better of you. You've never been in trouble with the law before. I'm sure the judge will look at you with sympathy. They always appreciate when somebody is extremely remorseful and confesses early on. It could easily mean a good few years off your sentence. If I were in your shoes, I'd confess now. Trust me, you'll feel way better. Your God will forgive you."

"I said, I don't know. Will somebody please tell me how Mary Kate is?"

Cullen ignored the question yet again and carried on as if he hadn't heard it.

"I suppose why you did it is irrelevant, but it could help your case. Listen to me, Jamie. You seem like a nice young lad. Do yourself a favour and unburden yourself. Would it help if there was a priest present?"

"When I said I don't know, I meant I'm not sure if I did it or not. I can't remember. I'd had an insane amount of drink. Lord

God, please watch over Mary Kate. Now, will somebody please tell me how she is?" This time, Jamie's voice was loud and aggressive.

Shit. Cullen felt that he might have overplayed the religious card, but having done their homework on this young man sitting opposite him, he felt it was the best way of getting through to him. He studied Jamie carefully, but he couldn't tell whether his hits were registering.

"Calm yourself down, boy, before I calm you down," interjected Detective Inspector Flood as he pushed his chair back and put his face into Jamie's.

Jamie had now been in the station for over six hours. Initially, he was kept in a cell with two uniformed guards who kept talking to him about nothing in particular. They had asked him a lot of questions but nothing specific to Mary Kate or what had happened. He had tried to pray for Mary Kate, but they kept on talking. It occurred to Jamie that they were there to keep him on his toes, to prevent him from having time to think.

Cullen and Flood had now arrived back, and the two young guards had left. Now, since the real questions started to register with him, he finally began to think of the situation that he was in. A wave of panic hit him, but he quickly regained his composure.

"Could I have a glass of water, please?" he asked as he felt his mouth go completely dry. He suddenly felt drained and thirsty. He hadn't had anything to eat or drink all day. Not that he had even thought of that up until now.

"Sure. No problem," replied Flood. He stood up and left the room.

"Jamie, think. Confess now and get it all over with. We know you did it. You know you did it. Why make it worse for yourself and everybody? Just tell the truth and shame the devil. Come on, son." Cullen looked straight into his eyes and put his hands over his hands. "Please, son. Make it easy for yourself."

"Will you please tell me how she is? If I did it, I would be the

32

THE TRUTH WILL OUT

first to confess, but I genuinely can't remember."

"So be it. I tried to help you," replied Cullen in a low voice, removing his hands from Jamie's hands.

Flood returned with a cup containing a yellowish liquid and handed it to Jamie.

"There's your water. Drink up."

Jamie put the liquid to his nose and was shocked by what he smelt.

"This is piss. You pissed into it," he shouted at Flood as he jumped to his feet. "What sort of an animal are you?"

"What sort of an animal am I? What sort of an animal am I? Christ, that's rich coming from a demented fuck like you," yelled Flood as he pushed the table at Jamie. As Jamie staggered backwards, he punched him full force in the stomach and pushed him to the ground.

"Here's your drink," Flood shouted as he threw the urine in Jamie's face. "Now, when you're quite finished, can you please come back to the table and answer our questions, if it's not too much trouble." Jamie turned and looked to Cullen for assistance, but Cullen merely shrugged his shoulders and gestured towards the chair.

At forty-four years of age, Flood had already served over twenty-five years in the guards. He had seen a hell of a lot of action in his time, and his reputation as a tough, no-nonsense cop was well deserved.

Of all the crimes he came across, the sexual offences were the ones he found the hardest to deal with. He had been lucky to date that there hadn't been that many of them, but with the current drug epidemic sweeping the country and hitting Dublin particularly hard, they were now on the increase.

Earlier that morning, when he had seen Mary Kate's beautiful lifeless body, Flood's thoughts had turned towards his own sixteen-year-old daughter. It had taken everything in his power to restrain himself from inflicting serious damage on Jamie. But now they were back on his turf.

Jamie sat down on the chair again, his head lowered into his chest.

As Flood started to talk, Jamie slowly lifted his head and stared directly into his eyes. Flood was momentarily taken aback. He had never seen such an evil look in all his life. He knew instantly that the young man behind those eyes was capable of anything, but before he had time to react, Jamie vaulted onto the table and kicked him in the side of the head. Even though he was over six foot tall and more than nine stone heavier than Jamie, the force knocked him to the floor.

"Don't fuck with me," said Jamie in a slow, determined voice as he calmly sat back down on his chair.

"Whatever you say," said Flood as he sat on his seat. He immediately reached out, grabbed Jamie by the hair and slammed his face into the table. Blood spurted from Jamie's nose as it was instantly broken. Flood then flung Jamie across the room and unleashed a flurry of punches, which knocked Jamie to the floor. Just as he threw back his leg to kick the prone figure, Cullen stepped in front of him.

"Come on, boss. Leave it out. We don't want a repeat of the last time. Remember?"

This seemed to take the steam out of Flood. He reached down, pulled Jamie to his feet by the hair, and hauled him back to the chair.

"Anything else you want to say?" After a brief moment of silence, he continued. "Good. Now, I would be very grateful if you could answer our questions if it's not too much of an inconvenience for you." His voice dripped with sarcasm.

Flood's head hurt, but there was absolutely no way he was going to let anyone know that. He also recognised the dangerous animal that he had sitting in front of him—a man who had no fear. Even now, as he looked at the bloodied face opposite him, Jamie was still staring straight back at him.

He knew exactly what Jamie would like to do to him.

"Don't look at me like that, boy. Otherwise, you'll get more of the same," Flood shouted as he thumped the table. At that moment, Cullen stood up and handcuffed Jamie to the chair.

As he did so, Jamie smiled.

Chapter 7

"LOOK, WE'VE BEEN over this time and time again. I don't know. I can't tell you something that I don't know. If I knew, I would tell you. I don't have the answers" replied Jamie, letting out a deep sigh.

It was now ten-fifteen p.m., and apart from visiting the toilet once at about five o'clock, he had not had a break from his interview with Cullen and Flood. He had given up asking about Mary Kate as they either refused to answer his questions or deliberately ignored them. He had not been provided with any food whatsoever, and he didn't dare ask for another glass of water. He knew that they were trying to break him, something that they would never do. But what concerned him most was that he couldn't answer their questions. In fact, Jamie was very slowly coming to the same conclusion that Flood and Cullen had come to. Had he had actually done it? He knew, when he totally lost it, he was indeed quite capable of nearly anything. But to attack and rape Mary Kate? Never. And not to be able to remember anything about it. It couldn't be. Could it?

"All right. Let's go over it again. Shall we?" Flood said. "Do you know a man named Peter Winterbottom?"

"Yes."

"And how do you know him?"

"He lives in the ground floor apartment opposite Mary Kate's. I've met him once or twice in the hall, as I've said every time you've asked me about him."

"Okay. Well, we received a 999 call from him this morning. He was walking by Apartment 1, Baggot Lane and—"

"Yes, I know," interrupted Jamie. "He noticed what appeared to be a woman lying on the floor. He took a closer look by peeping through the gap in the curtains and saw Mary Kate. Then he rang you guys. Right?"

"Don't be a smartarse. Can you please explain why the apartment was locked when we arrived?" said Flood.

"No. I can't."

"And there were no signs of forced entry?"

"If you say so."

"So, whoever attacked your good friend must have had access to her apartment," continued Flood.

"Again, if you say so," replied Jamie in a deadpan voice.

"I do say so," Flood said, but the tone of his voice gave the game away—he was struggling not to lose his temper. Jamie looked up at him and gave him a wry smile.

"Do you have a key for Mary Kate's apartment?"

"For fuck sake, for the hundredth time, yes, I have a key. Mary Kate gave it to me."

"Do you know if anybody else has a key?" interjected Cullen.

"As I've already said, as far as I know, the only people who have keys are Mary Kate, Shane Bradley, and me."

"Shane Bradley is her cousin and a very good friend of yours. Right?"

"Correct. God, you guys are good." Jamie smirked.

"Well, we know Mary Kate didn't rape herself, and we've located her key. Mr. Bradley walked her home last night and has his key, and you have kindly given us your key," said Cullen.

Cullen then ruffled through some papers on the table and, finding what he was looking for, continued. "According to Shane's statement," he said, appearing to be reading from it, "he arrived at the apartment at about three a.m. together with Mary Kate and his girlfriend, Julie Clarke. When they entered the apartment, they witnessed you passed out slumped over the kitchen table, clutching a bottle of Jameson. He asked Mary Kate if she wanted them to stay, given the state you were in, but Mary Kate—hold on, where is it?" He ran his finger down the page until he found the relevant section of Shane's statement. "Oh, yes, Mary Kate smiled and said that she would be okay and that you probably wouldn't stir until the morning. Shane asked her was she worried you would wake up, and she said that she would be able to handle you."

"But obviously not, huh?" said Flood as he sat back and waited for a reaction.

"Go on," said Jamie as he ignored Flood's comment.

Cullen continued, "So we know that you were the only person in the apartment with Mary Kate last night and that you had threatened her earlier...."

"For the last time, you shower of fuckwits, I didn't threaten her earlier." Jamie exploded and jumped to his feet. "I'm sorry. I didn't threaten her earlier," Jamie said as he regained his composure and sat down again.

"Careful of that temper of yours, sonny boy. It's already landed you in enough trouble" Flood laughed.

"According to numerous witnesses at the twenty-first birthday party you attended earlier that night, there was a major altercation between yourself and Mary Kate. She rejected your advances and humiliated you in front of everybody. You told her that you would 'get her' for that. Is that what you meant? That you would brutally assault and rape her, leaving her hanging onto life by a thread?" Flood said.

Jamie said nothing but a shudder of relief passed through him. This was the first time that he had heard that she was alive. He put his head into his hands, closed his eyes, and privately thanked God that she was alive. He prayed she would make a full recovery. Neither of the cops spoke as they waited for him to talk. They both thought they had finally hit a nerve and were waiting for the breakthrough. The confession.

"No. It wasn't like that," said Jamie. *Here we go,* Flood thought as he leaned in towards Jamie.

"Then tell us what it was like," whispered Cullen.

"Yes. I did have cross words with Mary Kate. But I don't think I told her I would 'get her.' I got extremely angry. I lost my cool, but I left to calm down. I know I fucked up, but I really don't think that I could hurt Mary Kate in any way. I just don't think I could have done it."

"Really? So throwing an empty beer keg through a window mightn't have hurt?" said Flood.

"I'm sorry about that. As I said, I lost my temper. I shouldn't have done that," replied Jamie.

"I'd say there were a lot of things you shouldn't have done that you're sorry about, son. Look, you should unburden yourself of all of it. Tell us exactly what happened. We know you didn't mean it," Cullen said, adding, "and you'll feel so much better."

Jamie looked up at the ceiling and screamed, "I can't remember. I can't remember. How can I say I did something if I don't know if I did it? Look, if I did it, I'd be the first to admit it and take my punishment."

"How can you say that you *didn't* do something if you don't know whether you did it or not?" Cullen said.

"Huh?"

"So, there is a possibility that you did it?"

Jamie thought for a moment before he looked at Cullen and replied, "Yes."

Cullen's heart began to pump a little faster. He felt they were finally getting somewhere.

"And since you were the only person in a locked apartment

40

with her, isn't it likely that you did it. I mean, nobody else could have done it," Cullen continued.

Again, "Yes."

"So, what you're saying is that, in all likelihood, you did it?" asked Cullen as he held his breath.

Silence. Both officers had been at this delicate stage on numerous occasions before and knew not to say another word. They waited for a reply. Jamie didn't speak for over a full minute, and when he did, it was almost in a whisper.

"I don't really think it is possible I did it and can't remember any of it. I know that it looks like I did it, but I would never harm a hair on Mary Kate's head. And not to be able to remember any of it! Like nothing at all! I just don't think it's possible," Jamie said to nobody in particular. It was as if he was talking to himself, trying to rationalise everything.

"I've had enough of this amnesia rubbish. You did it. You know you fucking did it, and you've invented this amnesia bullshit 'cause you know you can't answer the tough questions," Flood roared as he punched Jamie straight in the face. The force of the blow knocked Jamie off his chair. Cullen walked over and was helping him back to his feet when Flood charged at Jamie and slammed him against the back wall. He pulled him up by the ear and punched him in the midriff. The blow knocked the wind out of Jamie, and he struggled to regain his breath. Flood now towered over him and practically foamed at the mouth. Cullen stepped in front of Flood, shielding Jamie from him.

"Calm down, Dermot. This isn't helping anybody," he said as he gently pushed Flood backwards.

"Come on, Jamie, son. Sit back down there. Can I get you a glass of water or anything?" Cullen said as he righted the overturned chair and helped him back to his seat.

"You can do one thing for me please."

"What's that?"

"You can take these fucking handcuffs off me so the next time that elephant comes charging at me, maybe I might be able to defend myself. Or maybe your good friend, DETECTIVE INSPECTOR DERMOT FLOOD, gets off on beating up defenceless creatures about half his size. Eh? Is that your thing? Does that turn you on, Big Man? Eh?" Jamie taunted him, again looking straight into Flood's eyes. Flood stared straight back at him, and neither man flinched.

"Take off the handcuffs," Flood ordered Cullen, who duly obliged.

"Happy now?" Flood asked. "Look, Jamie. I'm sorry about what just happened there. I have a son your age, and believe it or not, I'm trying to help you. We know you didn't set out last night with the intention of harming anybody, let alone one of your best friends. By all accounts, the two of you were very close. But, apart from Mary Kate, have you given any thought to her family? Can you imagine how they are feeling right now? As we speak, they're holding a vigil at the hospital, praying she will wake up and not need all the machines that are keeping her alive at the moment. Praying that she will open her eyes and that she may breathe by herself. Jamie, they are absolutely devastated. But, on top of all that, to know that you don't have the courage to admit what you've done, that you're such a coward you don't even have the decency to say sorry for what you've done. Jamie, admit what you've done. At least do that much for Mary Kate, for her family. Please, Jamie, admit what you've done, for the love of God."

Jamie placed his head into his hands and began to weep. Slowly, his body began to shake as his sobs grew louder and louder. He couldn't stop the tears and, for the first time in his young life, had made no attempt to stop them. He was now crying uncontrollably. The two detectives again looked at each other in anticipation, hoping, this time, they would get the confession they knew would seal the case.

For three minutes, the only sound in the room was that of Jamie's weeping. Suddenly, he stopped and rose to his feet stretching his arms to heaven.

"Please, Lord Jesus, save me from this Hell. My Lord, my God, save me," he yelled.

"Save yourself, son. Tell us what happened," said Cullen softly.

"I can't."

Chapter 8

CULLEN FINALLY BROKE the silence in the interview room after what seemed like thirty minutes but, in reality, was probably only about five minutes.

"Jamie, it's nearly midnight now, and I think we should suspend the interview. Maybe you might remember more in the morning after you've had a good night's sleep. What do you think?"

Jamie didn't reply and stayed staring at the floor. He sat immobile, his head in his cupped hands. Neither detective could even hazard a guess as to what he was thinking, but they had decided not to interrupt him. They both hoped the confession that they so dearly required was imminent. From experience, they knew it was best to give the perpetrator time at this critical stage, time to think, time to worry.

The confession would seal the case. The evidence against Ryan was overwhelming, but it was by and large, circumstantial. Flood knew from bitter experience that one of those overpaid, smartarse lawyers would be able to drive a bus through it. There was no actual physical evidence that Ryan had done the deed, and there was a good chance—no, an excellent chance—a jury wouldn't convict. But the confession would change everything. And he was going to get his confession.

"Anyway, we should have some of the results back from the lab in the morning. That will throw some more light on it," Cullen continued as he stood up and headed out of the room.

As he pushed the door open, Jamie muttered, "What did you say?" without moving from his position.

"He said they'd have some of the results back from the lab. That will help us with our investigation," Flood said as he looked at Cullen. Maybe they were onto something.

"What's your blood type?" Cullen asked Jamie.

"I don't know."

"Are you prepared to give us a blood sample?"

"Sure. Just ask your gorilla friend here to wipe it from his knuckles," Jamie said as he took his head out of his hands and smiled at Flood.

Flood was just about to answer when Jamie continued, "Only joking. I have no problem giving a blood sample. Is that all the lab test for?

"Obviously, we also do fingerprints. The lab tests for many, many things apart from blood, and they will all help us. For starters, there's also the semen that we obtained from the rape kit and…"

"Ye guys are able to analyse semen! I didn't know that," Jamie interrupted.

"Yes, we can," Cullen replied.

Silence.

More Silence.

Both detectives stared at Jamie and tried to figure out what was going on in his head, where next to go with this.

"What can that tell you?" Jamie asked.

"Believe me, sonny, it can tell us a hell of a lot," answered Flood.

The detective was bluffing now, but maybe this would be the

trigger for the confession. He had recently been on a training course on the latest developments in forensic science and its enormous potential in criminal investigations. Researchers believed that semen was much the same as fingerprints, in that it was unique to an individual. They were in the process of developing the technology that would be capable of analysing any trace of semen left behind at a crime scene and matching it to an individual. But, as things stood, the technology was only in its infancy and couldn't tell anything. Detectives were encouraged to collect samples from crime scenes anyway in the hope that one day the technology would catch up and be able to positively match samples to the perpetrators.

But Jamie didn't know what Flood knew, and he decided to seize the opportunity.

"If you confess now before the results come back, it will look very good for you in court. We'll be able to tell the judge that you cooperated fully with us, that you were extremely remorseful, and that you confessed at the earliest opportunity," Flood said. He paused briefly and then continued. "If you don't confess, and we have to wait for the results to come back from the lab, he'll throw the book at you. It could be the difference of ten years. What age are you now, twenty? You could be out before you turn thirty with your whole life ahead of you. Don't be a fucking idiot. You're going down anyway. Why not make life easier for yourself? It will also help your family, as well as Mary Kate's family if you confess. In time, they will forgive you. We know it was totally out of character, and you didn't mean it to happen. But it did happen, and now you have to deal with it."

"What Detective Inspector Flood is saying makes sense, Jamie. You know it does. Think about it," Cullen said as he leaned over and placed his hands over Jamie's hands.

"I can't think. I need time to think. I can't think. I can't think." Jamie began shouting as he again put his head into his hands. His body began to shake, and his head started to pound as he digested what Flood had told him. He didn't know that they could do such things. He knew about fingerprints, of course, but analysing blood and semen?

"Can they really do that?" Jamie looked up at Cullen but immediately regretted asking the question. He knew he would be none the wiser after Cullen answered. Cullen would lie to him if need be. Also, by merely asking the question, it would further confirm his guilt in their eyes. Jamie knew he had to get his act together and to be very careful in everything he did and said now. The stakes were very high, and he couldn't afford any stupid moves. He was very tired and hungry, and he needed time to think. That's it. He decided there and then he wasn't going to say anything else until he had some time to himself. It also occurred to him that, with everything going on, he hadn't thought of Mary Kate in a while. More importantly, he hadn't prayed for her.

"Yes, Jamie, they can," Cullen answered.

"How is Mary Kate?"

"The last we heard was she is in intensive care and fighting for her life," Flood said. The words shocked Jamie. He immediately placed his head into his hands and began muttering to himself. But it wasn't exactly muttering—it was like chanting. The two detectives listened carefully and could just make out the low, droning chant now coming from the prisoner.

"Lord God Sweet Jesus, please save her."

"Lord God Sweet Jesus, please save her."

"Lord God Sweet Jesus, please save her."

"Lord God Sweet Jesus, please save her."

Over and over and over. The tears started to flow again.

"I've had enough of this shit. Let's wrap it up for the night. We'll talk again in the morning. I'll be back in a minute, Dave," said Flood as he left the room.

Cullen searched for the right thing to say to Jamie but, instead, walked over behind him and put his hands on both of his shoulders.

"Come on, son. Pull yourself together."

Jamie didn't respond, and Cullen continued. "This is helping nobody. Stop crying and pull yourself together. Would it help if you spoke to a priest?" He began to gently rock Jamie back and forth.

Flood returned to the room and, on seeing Cullen and Jamie, shrugged his shoulders, and looked up to heaven.

"Ah, isn't that lovely. Sorry to break up the party, but I'm also tired, and I want to go home to the wife and kids. On your feet, boy," he said.

Jamie continued praying and didn't acknowledge Flood's command.

"I said, ON YOUR FEET, BOY." Flood had had enough. He grabbed Jamie by the hair and pulled him to his feet.

"I don't like repeating myself. I need all your clothes, as well as your shoes and socks. Here's a blanket," he said as he threw a threadbare blanket into Jamie's face. "You'll be held in Cell No. 2 for tonight, and we'll talk first thing in the morning again. Now hurry the fuck up with those clothes." He started to put on a pair of rubber gloves.

Jamie looked up at him and asked, "Why do you need my clothes?"

"Suicide risk. Standard procedure, sonny. Now once you're stripped naked, I need you to bend over as I have to search your anal passage," Flood said, smiling at Jamie.

"What the fuck is that about?" Jamie replied in a raised voice. Flood could see the fear in Jamie's eyes as he looked to Cullen for assistance. Jamie knew instantly that Cullen wouldn't be able to help him.

"Suicide risk," repeated Flood.

Jamie now stood naked in front of him, his small frame starting to shiver from the cold.

"I said bend over. I also stated I don't like repeating myself, you scrawny little git. We could do this the easy way or the hard way. Your call, boy!" Flood shouted as he walked towards Jamie.

Jamie took a step back and glared at Flood. Flood knew this would provoke a reaction and was ready for him. Jamie also knew that Flood was goading him.

Game on, Jamie thought.

Jamie suddenly took another two steps backwards, turned quickly away from Flood and bent over. With his two hands, Jamie then separated his buttocks and let out a loud laugh.

"There you go, *sir*. Knock yourself out," Jamie screamed at the top of his voice.

Chapter 9

THE LIFE SUPPORT machine sustaining her life bleeped softly as Shane whispered into her ear, gently stroking her hair with one hand.

"I'm sorry. I am so sorry. I should never have left you. I just didn't think that Jamie would ever hurt you."

Mary Kate lay peacefully on the hospital bed surrounded by her immediate family and Shane. The doctors had earlier informed them that she had suffered severe blunt force trauma to the head, and it was impossible at this stage to know the full extent of her injuries. The next twenty-four hours would be critical, and the medics did not hold out much hope. Even if she did survive, she could be permanently brain damaged. To what extent? They couldn't get a clear answer to their questions.

Shane felt so helpless and guilty. There was absolutely nothing he could do now for Mary Kate. But when she had needed him, he wasn't there for her. He had let her down. Let her down badly. He had contemplated staying the night with Mary Kate when he dropped her home after the party. But NO. He had been too selfish. His girlfriend Julie had made it very clear to him earlier that 'tonight was the night', and he was on a promise. Julie's flatmate had gone home to Cork that afternoon—they would have the place to themselves for the whole weekend. He had actually asked Mary Kate if she wanted him to stay, but it was a half-hearted gesture, and she had known that.

The truth of it was that he didn't think for one second Mary Kate was in any danger. Jamie would come to in the morning. He would be mortified by his behaviour at the party. Shane would make him apologise. The fucking idiot. He had made up his mind that he was going to talk to Jamie about his drinking. God, he turned into such an asshole with too much drink on him. He knew that he would have to handle the conversation delicately, but he also knew that Jamie would listen to him.

They never got to have that conversation.

"I'm sorry, Uncle Joe. I should have protected her." Shane turned towards Mary Kate's father, the tears yet again running down his face. He had spent the day apologising to Mary Kate's family.

"You weren't to know. As I said to you earlier, it's not your fault. Please stop beating yourself up. No good will come of it. I don't blame you," Mary Kate's father replied as he once again embraced Shane.

Shane looked over at his Aunt Jane. She didn't move and stayed staring at the floor. Shane knew she blamed him. However, the fact of the matter was she hadn't heard a word that was said. She was lost in her own grief. How could this have happened to her baby? Her beautiful baby? Well, nothing like this would ever happen to her again, Jane swore to herself. She would take Mary Kate home and nurse her back to full health—that's what she'd do. Mary Kate would make a complete recovery, and she would have her beautiful baby back. She would never let any harm come to her again. Never.

"Aunt Jane? Aunt Jane? Please…"

Mary Kate's older brother moved closer to his mother. "Leave her be, Shane. Just drop it. Nobody's blaming you. All right? Now let's move on. We all know who's to blame."

At that moment, there was a small, hesitant knock on the door. Before anybody could answer, Jamie Ryan's parents, Dan and Mary, slowly opened it and entered the room. Both sets of parents had always been close friends as well as neighbours. That was partly why Jamie and Mary Kate were so close—they had practically grown up together. The two families had often holidayed together.

Mary took one look at Mary Kate lying there on the bed, pale as a sheet and covered in tubes and sensors, and immediately burst into tears.

She was like a daughter to her.

"Jane, Joe, we are so sorry…" Dan started to say.

"What are you people doing here? Don't you think you've caused enough trouble already?" Patrick shouted. He strode across the small room and began shoving Dan back towards the door.

"Patrick, we are so sorry for what has happened—" Dan started to say before Patrick again cut him short.

"Save it."

"Enough, Patrick. They're not to blame," said Joe as he gently pushed his son away from Dan.

"Thank you for coming. I know this is very hard for ye also," Joe continued as he hugged Dan and then Mary. "Please come in and take a seat."

Patrick looked at his father and then at Mary Kate and roared, "I'm not playing your little games. This is bullshit. Dad, look at her. Look at what their bastard of a son has done to her. And all you can say is 'please come in and take a seat.' Bullshit." He slammed the hospital door as he stormed out.

"I'm sorry about that. He's just—"

"No need to apologise, Joe. How is she?" Dan asked.

"We don't know. They won't tell us anything. All we know, Dan, is she is fighting for her life," Joe replied as his voice began to quiver.

"Oh, my God," whispered Mary as she looked at her good friend Jane. Jane ignored her and continued staring at Mary Kate.

"Jane, I'm so sorry," said Mary as she walked towards her with her arms outstretched to give her a hug.

"NO. Please don't do that," Jane shouted. "What are you doing here anyway?"

"Now, Jane, come on, please," said Joe. "Don't be like that. Dan and Mary just came—"

"Came to what? Came to ease their guilty conscience? Is that what you were going to say, Joe? You always said that no good would come of that boy, that you couldn't work it out, but there was something sinister about him. He was bad from the start. And now look what he's done to my beautiful baby." Jane broke down sobbing uncontrollably.

"I'm sorry, but I think it would be a good idea if you left now," Joe said as he held his wife. "We do appreciate you coming."

Mary looked at Mary Kate, blessed herself and left the room in a hurry, the tears rolling down her face. Dan looked from Jane to Joe and then to Mary Kate. She looked as if she was in a deep sleep, Dan thought. He was about to give her a kiss on the forehead, but he thought better of it. He turned to catch up with his wife.

"Wait," Joe said as he closed the hospital door behind him. "Jane is not herself at the moment. It's all such a terrible shock. We don't blame you," he said as he grabbed Dan's arm. He looked down at the ground as he asked, "Have you spoken to him yet? Did he say why?"

"No. The police came this morning asking loads of questions. They searched his room and spoke at length to the boys. We haven't heard anything from anybody since they left the house this afternoon," Dan replied. As he spoke, Patrick brushed by them without saying a word and went back into the room.

"Why would he do such a thing? Did he give any reason?" Joe

asked, but this time, the question was not addressed to anybody in particular. He was really struggling to make any sense of what had happened.

Shane appeared at his side. "Dan, Mary," he said as he nodded towards them. "Have you had a chance to talk to him yet?" Shane whispered.

"No, Shane, we haven't. Our thoughts have been with Mary Kate since we heard the news," Dan replied.

"Do you know what happened, Shane?" Mary said. "He worships Mary Kate. He would never hurt her, would he?" It wasn't so much a question from a loving mother but more of a plea.

Shane wasn't sure whether he was meant to answer her. The truth was he had been asking himself the same question all day, and he couldn't answer it. Jamie was his best friend. He knew that Jamie was capable of violence if he lost his temper. But it had been years since he had given in to his temper. He had learnt successfully to control it. And he had never been violent towards women. But could he have attacked Mary Kate? Raped Mary Kate? Left her for dead? He just couldn't believe that he could do it. But what he didn't know was whether he couldn't believe it or that he didn't want to believe it.

Before he could speak, Jamie's father answered his wife.

"Now look, Mary, the facts speak for themselves. We know he did it, and the sooner we accept that the better. What we have to do now is focus on Mary Kate."

Chapter 10

"I love you, Lord, my strength, my rock, my fortress, my saviour. My God is the rock where I take refuge; my shield, my mighty help, my stronghold. The Lord is worthy of all praise: when I call, I am saved from my foes."

JAMIE RYAN'S BRUISED body lay in the foetal position in a dark corner of his damp cell. He couldn't stop shivering from the cold. All he had left now were his prayers. He had many unusual prayers. If he heard a prayer at Mass or at a retreat that pricked his conscience, it had the power to overwhelm him. He would immediately set about committing that prayer to memory, to be called upon if required. The prayer he recited now was one of his favourites.

He had lost track of time but was fairly certain he had been in the Garda Station for at least three or maybe four days. He tried to think straight, to organise his thoughts, but he just couldn't manage it. He was starving, and his throat ached with thirst, but most of all, his body cried out for sleep. However, he tried his utmost to stay awake. They wouldn't win. They wouldn't break him.

"I love you, Lord my strength," he whispered. He could fight no longer. He slept.

"Jamie, wake up there, lad."

Not again. Please no, not again.

Jamie was once again dragged from his sleep by the guard.

"Just checking you're okay," the guard continued, gently and repeatedly slapping Jamie's face. He then shook his head to make sure he was awake.

"Would you like a drink of water?"

Jamie looked at him blankly. He had vague memories of the past few days, of why he was here. He couldn't remember the last time he had slept. The days and nights were all blurring into one. He recalled first entering the cell, only to find there was no bed or mattress for him to sleep on. He had said it to the guard on duty who informed him that he would get it sorted. He had waited for him to return, but he never did. Eventually, he wrapped the threadbare blanket they had given him around himself and lay on the hard, damp floor. Then... What happened next? He couldn't recall. His cell door opening and closing; lights flickering on and off; guards coming and going; slaps, kicks, punches. On the first night—or was it the second?—he was woken up by somebody pulling him by the hair. There were four or five of them in his cell. They had wet, twisted towels and they proceeded to whip him with them. He heard one guard telling the others to be careful not to bruise him too much. Had that actually happened? Or was his mind playing tricks on him?

He realised fairly quickly that they didn't want him to sleep. Jamie was determined not to give them the satisfaction of beating him. He struggled to stay awake. But he couldn't manage it anymore. By now, he thought his head was going to explode.

"Please, guard, just let me sleep."

"No problem, Jamie. I was just checking on you."

He closed his eyes again and slept.

They would let him sleep now. But only for five minutes. They knew what they were doing. Their prized confession was near.

Splash!

As they had done on previous occasions, they announced morning time by throwing a freezing cold bucket of water over his naked body. He jumped up with the shock.

"Rise and shine, son. It's morning time. Sleep well?" It was his old friend Detective Inspector Dermot Flood.

"Fuck you," whispered Jamie.

"My, my. Aren't we in a bad mood this morning?" Flood laughed.

"What time is it?" Jamie yawned.

"Time for breakfast. You want some?" Flood replied.

"Yes, please."

"No worries. Get yourself dressed," Flood said as he threw Jamie the clothes that they took off him every night. The suicide risk routine. Jamie was sure Flood took great pleasure in strip-searching him every night.

As usual, breakfast never arrived, and once again, he had spent the day being interviewed by Cullen and Flood.

"Are you going to charge me?"

"Charge you with what? What did you do? Flood replied.

It was now evening, after an endless day of relentless interrogation, and Jamie was completely exhausted. He was given a little food and water earlier in the day, but he felt lightheaded with the hunger. The sleep deprivation was really taking its toll on him, and now he just wanted it all to end. He didn't care anymore.

"Have you something you want to tell us?"

"Look. I've already told you everything. I can't remember. How long can you keep me here like this?" Jamie asked as he once again broke down. He was deeply ashamed of himself. He had been so proud all his life that, in spite of his size, he could more than look after himself. And now he was blubbering like a baby. Again.

"As long as I fucking well like, you little dipshit," Flood

replied as he slapped Jamie hard across the face. "Stop thinking of yourself. Think of Mary Kate and what you did to her. Think of her family, your family—"

"Enough. Game over. You win!" Jamie leaned over the table and stared into Flood's eyes.

"Give me five minutes on my own to make peace with my Maker, and I'll tell you everything. Deal?" His face now in Flood's face.

The two guards looked at each other.

"Five minutes," Flood replied. "That's it. And you better not be dicking me around, or there'll be hell to pay." The two men stood up to leave the room.

"Five minutes, Jamie. Good, lad. Son, you're doing the right thing," Cullen added as they closed the door, leaving Jamie alone to his thoughts.

Jamie now considered his options for the last time. He knew he couldn't take much more, but he had also been thinking about what the guards had said to him.

Mary Kate had always been very security conscious; she would not have answered the door to anybody after Shane had left her home. He knew this from experience—he had called one night, drunk and looking for a place to crash, and there was no answer no matter how many times he pressed the buzzer. He had walked the streets until the buses started running in the morning, then headed off home. She informed him the next day that she never answers her door after dark. That day she got a key cut for him.

"There you go. You can crash anytime. Save me bricking myself when the buzzer goes off in the middle of the night," she had said, laughing, and handing him his key that evening.

Jamie also knew that there was a dark side to him, a side he concealed from everybody. He could have bad thoughts—no, pure evil thoughts—that could jump into his mind at any time. He might be listening to somebody; maybe a boring uncle droning on and he'd think to himself, *I wonder if I hit him with a claw hammer on the back of the head, what would it sound like? Would his skull crack on the first or second blow?* Of course, he never even contemplated acting on these thoughts, but sometimes, his own mind frightened him. He had never discussed them with anybody other than God. He prayed to make them go away.

He had also lost control of his temper that night. Jamie had not allowed that to happen for a very long time as he was well aware that there were always consequences when he did lose control. Severe consequences.

But why couldn't he remember? Could he have done it and not remember? It seemed implausible that he wouldn't remember. No, not implausible, unbelievable. They were right—it was unbelievable. And if he didn't do it, was it believable that he had either slept through the attack or that he couldn't recall the attack. His head ached as he struggled to make sense of the chaos in his brain.

"Well?" Flood said as the detectives re-entered the interview room.

"In thee, O Lord, I put my trust."

"What the fu—?"

"Yes. That's it. That's it. Oh, how did I miss it? Why did it take me so long?" Jamie smiled as he spoke to the detectives.

"I was blind, but now I see."

"Look, Jamie, you had better quit with this religious bullshit—" Flood started to say, but Cullen cut across him.

"What is it, Jamie? What do you see?"

Jamie reached out and cupped his hands around Cullen's.

Jamie now finally realised what the Lord had wanted him to do. He had been too busy fighting with the detectives to see what the Lord had planned for him. This wasn't about Mary Kate. This was a test for him. A test that he had nearly failed.

When I call, I am saved from my foes.

He had misunderstood. Flood and Cullen weren't his foes. Alcohol was his foe, and it brought him to this place. It had the

61

power over him, and the Devil was working through it. But the Lord God was testing him, testing his faith.

He now understood the test. There was a reason that Mary Kate was still alive, and only he could save her now. He had to put his complete faith in the Lord God. Only He would save him from his foes. He would never drink again. He promised that to God there and then. This was a wake-up call from God. He would pass the test and save her. After the merciful Lord spared her life, she would then be able to tell them the truth.

Jamie now faced the ultimate test of his faith. He was euphoric. He also knew that this would bring the madness to an end, and he would be granted sleep. That idea alone was nearly enough.

"I would like to confess to the ra—, to the assault on Mary Kate."

"So finally you're admitting that you did it?" Flood said.

Jamie thought carefully before replying.

"As I said, I confess to the assault on Mary Kate."

Chapter 11

Behold, God is my salvation; I will trust, and not be afraid: for the Lord Jehovah is my strength and my song; He also has become my salvation.

JAMIE PLACED HIS left hand on the wrist of his right hand in order to stop it from shaking. He kept telling himself he was doing the right thing. His mind was made up.

Lord, my strength, my rock, my fortress, my saviour...

They had promised him—he had even made them swear it—they would leave him alone; he would be allowed sleep.

"Do you want me to read it to you again?" Cullen asked.

"No. I'll sign it," he replied.

...my shield, my mighty help, my stronghold...

It was now 9.32 p.m., about forty-five minutes after he had first confessed. Things had moved very quickly since then. After he had confessed, he initially refused to do or say anything further until they let him sleep. But they wouldn't agree to that until they had a signed, written confession.

"Trust me, Jamie. You'll feel so much better after you've made a full confession," Cullen had said. A compromise was reached when Cullen suggested that they would send out for some food—cheeseburger and chips and a can of coke—and he could eat it while they took his confession. Reheated chips had never tasted so good.

The confession itself didn't take very long. Obviously, Jamie had never been in a position before in his life where he had had to make a formal confession. He didn't know where to start.

"How about I help you? I'll call out some of the basics, and you write it down, okay?" Flood asked. Jamie nodded his agreement but couldn't contain his laughter when Flood started.

"I, Jamie Ryan, being of sound mind, over the age of eighteen and under my own volition. What's so funny?" Flood stopped and shouted at him.

"Nothing. Sorry, carry on, sir," Jamie replied. He was now more determined than ever to extract himself from his present predicament. There's no point prolonging this anymore, he told himself.

His confession ran to a little over three pages. It was all in his handwriting, and he had made no changes to what Flood had called out to him. The earlier part of the confession, covering all that had happened at the party and how Jamie had ended up back in Mary Kate's apartment, had gone very smoothly. However, when it came to the actual assault and rape of Mary Kate, Flood stopped talking, waiting for Jamie to say in his own words exactly what had happened. But Jamie just looked at Flood when he fell silent.

"I think it would be best at this stage if you told us exactly how it happened, Jamie" interjected Cullen.

"It's working fine so far. Carry on," replied Jamie.

"All right, then," said Flood as he shrugged his shoulders. "Where were we? Oh, yes. I used the key that I had to Mary Kate's apartment to let myself in. I was still absolutely livid with her for humiliating me the way she did at the party in front of everybody. I decided she would pay for it. I knew that somebody, more than likely Shane Bradley, would drop her home later. She would never come home at night by herself. I pretended to be passed out drunk on the kitchen table when they arrived and waited until we were alone and I was certain Shane had left. Then I confronted her about what happened earlier."

Flood paused again and looked expectantly at Jamie, but Jamie simply returned the stare. For a long moment, they both just stared straight into each other's eyes, each expecting the other to take up the story.

Flood finally broke the silence. "I really think you should take it from here."

Jamie Ryan shook his head slowly. "I told you I would confess, and I will. This way is working. Please continue." He knew the futility of telling them yet again that he couldn't remember anything of what happened in Mary Kate's apartment that night.

Flood then looked over at Cullen, and then continued. "She told me I behaved like an idiot earlier, and she had decided that she didn't want anything to do with me anymore. She said that sometimes I scared her and that I was scaring her now. She then asked me to leave. She told me that if I didn't, she would call the police. I laughed at her, but the next second, she started screaming for help. I went to put my hand on her, to calm her down, but she went mental. That's when she slapped me across the face. I tried to remain calm, but I could feel the rage building up inside of me. I tried to talk to her in a calm voice but, when I began to speak, she started screaming hysterically and slapping and punching me."

Flood stopped again, and looked from Jamie to Cullen, "Jamie, you have to take it from here."

"No."

"You must."

"No, carry on. Let's get this over with."

"Jesus, you really don't remember, do you?" asked Flood as he again looked over at Cullen.

Before Jamie could reply, Cullen jumped in. "Right, Jamie,

let's carry on then. I lost it totally, and before I knew it, I had hit Mary Kate a full punch to the face. She immediately hit the floor and began whimpering. I told her to shut up and stay quiet because I couldn't think straight, I was so angry. I remember her then getting up and going towards the phone. She didn't say anything, but I knew I had totally blown everything. I knew she was going to call the guards. I think that's when I totally lost it."

The room fell silent yet again.

Cullen continued. "It's all a bit of a blur, but that's when I raped her. She didn't really struggle much. It was like I was looking at somebody else doing this horrendous deed, even though I knew it was me. When I was finished, I stood over her and told her she wasn't so smart now. I saw the utter contempt she had for me when she told me 'we'll see who's so clever when you go to prison for this. A lovely cute little boy like you, you'll make somebody's pretty bitch in there, and we'll see how you like it.' She spat the words at me. It was then I knew she couldn't live, and I picked up the ..."

Cullen paused and asked Jamie.

"What was it you hit her with again, Jamie?"

"I'm not sure. You tell me."

"Surely, you know, Jamie. Surely, you remember what you hit her with," Cullen pressed.

"Look," Jamie raised his voice. "I just want this to end. End now. So tell me what I hit her with, and I'll write it down. Okay? I'll stick to my part of the deal, you stick to yours."

"Okay. I hit her with the poker from the fire. Hit her hard a number of times. There was blood everywhere. I was sure she was dead," Cullen concluded.

Jamie continued to write, not looking up at either of the two detectives.

"That's it?" he asked when he was finished writing.

"Yes," replied Cullen. "Not unless you have anything else to add."

Jamie started writing again.

"Finished," he then said as if he were doing an exam. He handed the signed statement to Flood.

It was done. Now they would leave him be, and he could sleep. He had placed his destiny in the hands of the Lord and would accept the consequences of his actions. The truth would save him. Mary Kate would save him.

At the back of his mind, he thought about his 'Trump Card' and whether it would stack up or not.

Flood and Cullen read what Jamie had written at the end of his statement.

"I am sorry for my sins. In thee, O Lord, I put my trust."

Chapter 12

"ALL RISE. THE Right Honourable Judge Maura Walsh presiding."

Twenty-two days had now passed since Jamie Ryan signed his confession and life had changed utterly for him. His previous carefree life was a distant memory.

The two detectives had been as good as their word and had honoured their side of the deal. He was allowed uninterrupted sleep for all of that night. The next morning, he was formally charged with the rape and attempted murder of Mary Kate Quinn.

"Have you anything to say?" Flood had asked after he finished reading out the charges.

"Now I can only pray for Mary Kate. Please tell me how she is?" he replied.

That morning was a bit of a blur. Everything happened so fast. Jamie was taken out by the rear exit of the police station and bundled into the back of a waiting patrol car, wedged in the back seat between Flood and Cullen. The car was then driven at great speed, siren blazing, the short distance to The Four Courts. As they approached the court building, Cullen reached over and handed him a blanket.

"Here, take this."

"Why?" asked Jamie.

"Because of the media, you clown," replied Cullen.

"What are the media doing here?" asked Jamie. "Christ, there are a lot of them here," he added as he suddenly saw the large crowd of photographers jostling for position.

"Your crime of passion has attracted a lot of attention, my boy," said Flood. "Look, Jamie, sex crimes are very rare in Ireland. And, because of Mary Kate's grandfather, her picture has been all over the front pages. She was, sorry is, a beautiful looking woman."

"Her Grandfather?"

"Yes. Don't tell me you don't know who her grandfather was," said Flood.

"I think I met him once but what—" Jamie stopped in mid-sentence. It suddenly dawned on him that he had been a very high profile politician. In fact, if Jamie's memory served him right, he had previously been a Minister for Justice, well known as a harsh critic of the judicial system and its perceived soft attitude on crime.

"Bring back the birch," had been his motto. "There's no crime in The Isle of Man."

"Oh, I see," said Jamie as he took the blanket from Cullen. My God, he had seen it so many times on the news—people scurrying into court, trying to hide their faces. He never imagined that one day he would be doing the same.

But wait. No. He smiled at the detective and handed him back the blanket.

Aha, another test, My Lord. What will be will be.

"No. I don't want a blanket. I will meet whatever comes at me head on," Jamie said.

Jamie hadn't had much time to think since he had signed the confession. But now, after several hours sleep, he really wasn't sure if he had done the right thing. But, earlier that morning, with a clear head, he thought about the situation he was in and was of the firm belief that only God could save him. He had to put his complete and utter faith in God. If he did that, God would spare Mary Kate, and this madness would end. He had decided there was no going back, and he was not going to dwell on it any longer.

Sometimes, he questioned his own sanity, but the decision was made.

"Jamie, son. Are you sure? Please think about it. Your case probably won't come to trial for at least a year, and there's no reason why you won't get bail. You go out there now, and everybody will know your face. It won't be safe for you."

The car skidded to a halt. Jamie smiled at him and dropped the blanket on the floor of the car.

Seconds later, how he yearned for that blanket. Nothing prepared him for the media scrum that followed. Shouting, screaming, cameras flashing, people running towards him. Mayhem.

He walked resolutely between the two detectives. His heart was thumping so hard, it felt like it would burst out of his chest, his legs like jelly, he was sure they would no longer support him. But they did, and the detectives reached the sanctuary of the courthouse.

His first court appearance of his life lasted less than five minutes. Everything happened so quickly. The charges were read out in front of the judge, and before he had a chance to say anything, somebody jumped up from beside him and spoke on his behalf. He was granted free legal aid and remanded in Mountjoy prison for one week.

Today, over three weeks later, was his fourth court appearance. Today was special as it was the first time that his solicitor said that they would apply for bail. Jamie was still struggling to get his head around the mechanics of the legal system. Firstly, he was amazed just how long it would take for his case to come to trial.

"But I signed a confession," Jamie said to his solicitor, Tom

Dylan when Tom was patiently explaining it all to him.

"That may be, but the State must thoroughly prepare its case, its book of evidence. In some instances, it may take years before a case goes to trial. However, I would say, given your case has generated such media interest, they will fast track it. It may be heard within the next twelve to eighteen months."

"What happens to me in the meantime?" Jamie asked.

"We'll apply for bail. That means you will be released under certain conditions. Normally, they ask for a certain amount of money to be lodged into the court and also other pledges of money—they're called sureties—from other people to ensure that you'll turn up for your trial. The judge can apply whatever bail conditions he or she deems fit."

"But if I don't get bail?"

"Jamie, I think there's an excellent chance you'll get bail. There are very limited reasons why a judge can refuse bail—if they believe you might intimidate any witnesses, which doesn't apply in your case since there are no witnesses, or if you're seen as a flight risk. Jamie, our great legal system here in Ireland gives bail to murderers, armed robbers, rapists... Sorry, I didn't mean to imply that—"

"Don't sweat it, Tom. It's okay."

Initially, when Jamie had first met Tom, he was concerned at how young he looked. It transpired that Tom didn't just look young, he was young. At twenty-six years of age, he had qualified as a solicitor only in the last eighteen months. This was his third criminal case and his first for a really serious crime. Tom had explained to Jamie that, since Jamie did not have the financial resources to employ a solicitor to defend him, he was entitled to free legal aid from the State. Tom had been assigned to his case but was at pains to point out his own lack of experience. He reminded Jamie at every opportunity that he had the right to change counsel if he wanted and even went on to suggest another solicitor's name.

Jamie's first thoughts were to take Tom up on his offer. But then he realised nothing turned on the case. It was only a sideshow. When Mary Kate woke up, it would all be over. Tom actually seemed disappointed when Jamie informed him that he was happy to keep him on as counsel.

"Very well then," Judge Maura Walsh said after she listened to all the arguments. "I require the defendant to surrender his passport and to sign on weekly at Terenure Garda Station. Bail is set at £5,000 and two independent sureties of £10,000 each."

"But Your Honour," Tom addressed the court. "£5,000 is such a large sum of money. It is more than twice the average annual industrial wage. My client is a young man, a student, and would not be capable of raising such funds. He simply doesn't have access to that kind of money."

"That may be, but I understand that amount of money should not cause any major problems for his family. They are the conditions of his bail, Mr. Dylan. I will allow you one hour to see if the conditions can be met. We will reconvene at two p.m.," the judge finished as she rose to her feet.

Jamie was taken to a holding cell in the bowels of the court building while Tom set about attempting to meet the bail conditions. Jamie knew all was not right when Tom returned forty minutes later.

"Okay, Jamie, we have a problem. Your mother has said she'll deposit the £5,000 and also, she'll sign one of the independent sureties…"

"Right. So that's one. And Dad will sign the other one, so what's the problem? Jamie interrupted.

"I don't know how to say this gently, Jamie—your Dad won't do it," replied Tom.

"That's crazy. If he thinks I'm a flight risk, tell him—"

"No, it's not that. In fact, he gave me a message to give to you. He made me promise I would deliver it verbatim." Tom cleared his throat before continuing. "I'm sorry, Jamie. These are his words, not mine. He says that you are dead to him, and he hopes you rot in hell for what you did."

"Oh." Jamie experienced a strange sensation of the world shrinking around him. He had had the feeling that something was not right with his father as he hadn't come to visit him in prison. His mother had been his only visitor on visiting days. She had explained his father's absence by the fact that they would only allow one visitor. When he had asked about his father and the rest of his family, she was very coy and evasive in her replies.

"Is there anything else we can do?" Jamie finally asked. "To tell you the truth, Tom, I'm not the most popular guy in prison. I'm treated as a sex offender, and because of that, I'm locked up in that tiny cell twenty-three hours a day. They say it's for my own protection, and I believe them. I hear the other inmates shouting what they're going to do to me when they get their hands on me, and I'd say some of the screws—sorry, the prison officers, feel the same way. Can you persuade the judge to lower the bar?"

"That's our only option, but I wouldn't be too hopeful today," said Tom as he started gathering up his papers.

"One other thing, Jamie. Your mother's money is in a joint account with your father, and at the moment, he is refusing to sign the forms required to release the money. Your mother is working on it as we speak and will let me know before I address the judge again."

"Right," replied Jamie as he felt the tears well up in his eyes.

Chapter 13

"I AM SORRY, Mr. Dylan. For the reasons I have outlined to you already, those are the terms of Mr. Ryan's bail, and I will not alter them. I have heard your arguments and, quite frankly, they do not impress me. So, as things stand, you are in a position to post one of the sureties, and that's all you can do at the moment. Very well, I will put the case down for mention again in two weeks' time, the——"

"I'll do it," a voice called from the back of the court before the judge had a chance to finish. "I'll lodge the money and post the other surety."

There was an audible gasp in the courtroom as all eyes turned towards the voice.

"Silence. Silence in my court," Judge Walsh shouted as she banged her small wooden hammer. "This is most unusual. Most unusual, indeed. Young man, please step forward."

Shane Bradley walked hesitantly to the front of the court.

"Normally, young man, you are not permitted to address the court. Indeed, you could even be held in contempt of court. However, I will let it go. Tell me, do you have access to that amount of money? It is a very large amount."

"I am sorry, Judge... sorry, Your Honour. I didn't mean any disrespect to your court. Yes, I have over five thousand in cash. Unfortunately, my granny died last year and left me a lot of money."

"Objection, Your Honour. Even if this young man has the deposit, surely, he is not in a position to meet the surety if required." The prosecution counsel finally rose to his feet.

"Sit down, Mr. Smyth and kindly let *me* finish," said the judge sternly. Then, turning back to Shane, "The surety. Do you have the funds if called upon?"

"I don't have it all in cash at the moment, but I am sure I can raise it if need be," replied Shane as he looked over towards Jamie. This was the first time Jamie had seen Shane since that terrible night. Jamie averted his eyes, not knowing how to react.

"Very well. So be it," the judge replied.

"Your Honour, if it pleases the court, I have one other minor problem," Tom Dylan said.

"Mr. Dylan, you are testing my patience and the patience of this court. What is it now?"

"My client doesn't have a passport to surrender."

Chapter 14

"YOU DID WHAT?"

Shane's father, Tim, was shouting at him.

"For the love of God, Shane, why?"

"I don't really know, Dad. I hadn't intended to do it. It's just when I saw him there—"

"Shane, you can't do it. You can't do this to our family, to your mother and me," Tim interrupted him. "It's not too late. Just go back and say you can't raise the money or, better still, you've changed your mind."

"But, Dad—"

"But nothing, Shane. It's not right. Have you considered for one second the consequences of your actions? Have you thought about your Aunt Jane and Uncle Joe? How do you think will they feel? Please don't follow through with this madness. I'm begging you, Shane. It's not right."

None of Mary Kate's family had been at the hearing. The prosecutors had said they would oppose bail, but they thought he would probably get it. They just weren't sure how high the bar would be set. Nobody had anticipated Shane would play such a central role in today's proceedings. Shane now had to return to the court with a bank draft and sign up all the relevant paperwork. Once all of it was completed, Jamie Ryan would be released on bail.

"Dad, look, you know the way you always taught me not to be a sheep, to think for myself, and to make my own decisions in my life."

"Yes, Shane, I know. But please, not this. Don't you think my sister and her family have suffered enough? Her beautiful daughter lying there in the hospital bed as good as dead."

"We don't know that, Dad. Don't say that. Please don't say that," Shane said, a tear coming to his eye.

Tim looked at his son. He knew how hard all this had been on him. On the outside, Shane might look like a big strapping man, but he was still only a boy and a very sensitive one at that. Tim had cried all his tears by now. He'd resigned himself to the fact that Mary Kate would lose her fight for life. In his mind, it was only a matter of time. The doctors didn't hold out much hope. They weren't sure whether she would survive if the machines were switched off, and they had said it was extremely unlikely she would ever regain consciousness.

As the days had turned into weeks, Tim now thought it would be better for everybody if she were to die. If she lived, there was a very strong chance of permanent brain damage, the extent of which nobody knew for certain, but they feared the worst. The current situation was death by a thousand cuts, and he hated seeing how it was destroying his sister. At least if Mary Kate died, they would have closure. They could start rebuilding their lives, no matter how hard that would be.

"Okay, Shane. I'm sorry, but you're going to have to face facts. You've heard what the doctors have said. We've all heard them say it's extremely unlikely that she will ever regain consciousness."

"I know, Dad. I know what they say. But they're wrong. She can't die," Shane whispered. "And I know Jamie. I know him better than anyone else in the whole world. This is something I have to do. I have to talk to him. I have to find out what happened that night," Shane said, but this time in a strong voice.

"You can talk to him without doing this, Shane. You can visit him in prison if you want to. But you heard what the police said. He admitted it. He admitted what he did." Tim couldn't disguise the anger in his voice.

"Exactly, Dad. But something's not right. You were there when the police told us he had confessed. But the big guard—I can't remember his name—did you see how agitated he was? He couldn't even look Aunt Jane in the eye. What was all that about? You'd think they would have been more upbeat after Jamie finally confessed—they now had their man. But they looked a bit shifty to me. I'm telling you, something's not right."

"No, Shane, you're wrong. You're clutching at straws. I didn't notice anything about the guards. I would say they were probably just upset, seeing Mary Kate lying in the bed like that. You're making too much of it. And you're ignoring the fact that Jamie admitted that he did it—that he raped and attacked Mary Kate."

"But that's another thing, Dad," Shane replied. "If Jamie had done it, the very first thing he would have done would have been to admit it, and to say how sorry he was. It wouldn't have taken him four days. If he fucks up—sorry, Dad—screws up, he is the first to own up and face the music. That's the way he is."

"That may be, Shane, but what if this time, the consequences are just too big for him? Think of what he's done. It's not like breaking somebody's nose on a rugby pitch. Whether Mary Kate lives or not, he's still going to prison for a long time."

"But, Dad—"

"Shane, listen up. He did it. He admitted he did it. You also know everything there is to know about the case. Nobody else could have done it. He did it, and that's all there is to it."

"I have to talk to him. I have to do this, Dad. Please understand," Shane said.

"I don't understand," his father replied curtly.

"Look, that's it. I'm doing this thing, and that's all there is to it. I am truly sorry if it hurts you and Aunt Jane, but it's something I have to do. Believe me, it's not my intention to hurt anybody. Jamie's my best friend, and I have to find out what happened that night."

"It may not be your intention to hurt anybody, but you will," Tim said as he looked at his son. He knew there was no further point in continuing the conversation. Once Shane had made up his mind, he was not for turning.

However, Tim could see from Shane's demeanour that there was something else.

"Well, what else do you want to tell me? Spit it out, Shane. I know you too well," Tim said.

"I'm taking a break from my studies. I'm going to go off with Jamie and get to the bottom of this, no matter how long it takes," Shane replied.

"No, Shane. I forbid it. Do you hear me? You worked so hard to get into medical school," Tim protested.

"Dad, I'm only taking a break. It could only be for a few days or maybe a few weeks. I don't know. I'm sorry, Dad, but that's what I'm doing."

Tim looked at his son and realised the bravery of his decisions. Normally, he admired his son's quiet determination to follow his own path.

But now, he was making the biggest mistake of his young life, one which he would spend the rest of his life regretting. Mary Kate would die, and Jamie would be convicted of her murder. And the extended family would never forgive Shane for going against them. That is the way it would be perceived.

He also felt helpless because he knew nothing he or anybody else would say would have any impact on Shane's decision.

"Dad, I'm going over to the hospital now to tell Aunt Jane what I'm doing. I don't want to hide from this," Shane said.

"No, Shane, I'll tell her. She'll hear it from me, and that's the end of it. Go, do what you feel you have to do. For what it's worth, you don't have my blessing, and I think you're making a catastrophic mistake." Tim stood up and embraced his son.

"Thank you, Dad. I'm sorry," Shane whispered in his father's ear.

Chapter 15

"I HAVE TWO questions. But first, you must promise me—swear to me—- that you will answer them truthfully, no matter how hard the truth is. You at least owe me that. Swear?"

It was now after eleven p.m., and Jamie had been released on bail after five that evening. Tom Dylan had arranged for Shane to collect Jamie at the rear of the courthouse. Jamie ran the gauntlet of the media uncovered, but Shane sped away as soon as Jamie was inside the car.

The two men had said very little throughout the long journey.

"Thank you, Shane," Jamie had said once they had left the media behind.

"We'll talk later, Jamie," Shane replied. "I've rented a small cottage in the back of beyond, Clifden, in Connemara to be precise, and we'll talk when we get there. I don't want to do this in the car."

Neither man was interested in small talk so the journey had passed mostly in silence. About halfway, they stopped at a pub for a bite to eat. However, as they were about to take their seats, a man, clearly with a lot of drink on him, stumbled over.

"You, I recognise you from the telly. You're the scumbag that attacked that young one in Dublin, aren't you?" he shouted, leaning in towards Jamie. "Hanging is too good for the likes of you," he continued, warming to his subject. "You should have your balls cut off with a rusty blade."

Shane quickly positioned himself between Jamie and the drunk.

"Take it easy there, friend. I think you've mistaken him for somebody else," he said calmly.

The drunk looked hard at Jamie and then at Shane. After a few seconds, he shook his head and said, "Sorry about that. You sure look a hell of a lot like that little wanker." He turned on his heels and shuffled off.

However, by now, the pub had fallen silent, and all eyes were on Jamie.

"I think we better go," Shane said as he grabbed his coat, and both young men beat a hasty retreat.

"Not one of your brighter ideas that," Shane said after they had travelled a few miles from the pub.

"What do you mean?" Jamie asked, puzzled by Shane's statement.

"The whole 'see-this-face' routine with the cameras," Shane replied, and he made an impression of Jamie staring menacingly at the cameras.

"I think you're right," Jamie admitted.

"You think!" Shane replied and, with that, both of them started to laugh. At first, it was only a small laugh, but it then developed until both of them were laughing hysterically, so much so, Shane had to pull the car over. It was such a release of tension after all the events of the past few weeks.

However, once they managed to compose themselves, the rest of the journey continued in silence.

Shane and Jamie were now sitting down opposite each other across a kitchen table in their rented cottage. Shane hadn't exaggerated when he said they were going to a remote spot. The cottage was up a narrow lane, about seven miles outside the small village of Clifden, in the far west of the country. The nearest dwelling was over two miles away.

Shane opened two bottles of Smithwicks beer from a six-pack he had brought along. He was now waiting patiently for Jamie to answer him, to swear that he would tell him the truth. Jamie was taking his time to reply and avoiding eye contact, but Shane had no intention of saying another word, no matter how uncomfortable the silence became.

"I swear," Jamie eventually replied.

Shane had been very deliberate in his choice of words. He was fully aware of Jamie's deeply held religious beliefs—he knew how strongly Jamie felt about swearing to anything. He had considered getting him to swear on the Holy Bible but had decided against it.

"Thank you," said Shane, and he took a deep breath. But just before he started to ask his questions, he suddenly realised that he was totally unprepared for the answers. During the car journey, he had rehearsed over and over in his mind how he was going to approach this conversation, but he had given no thought as to what Jamie's answers could be. What would he do if his worst fears were realised? Anyway, there was no turning back now.

"Did you do it?" he finally asked.

"Shane." This time, it was Jamie's turn to take a deep breath. "You are my best friend. Believe me when I say that, apart from Mary Kate's recovery, there is absolutely nothing in this whole wide world that would make me happier than to be able to tell you that I didn't do it. But the truth of the matter is I have no memory of what actually happened that night. I mean, I can remember making a complete gobshite out of myself at the party and going back to Mary Kate's apartment, having more whiskey back there, but that's it. The next thing I remember is waking up on the floor with the cops in the room."

"Could it be that you blocked it out of your mind?" Shane asked.

"Is that your second question?" Jamie jokingly asked.

"No, it's not, Jamie. Don't be a dickhead. This ain't no laughing matter," Shane replied. He was very taken aback by Jamie's casual attitude. Could it be?

"I'm sorry, Shane. I didn't mean to be making a joke out of this. Honest, I didn't. It's just the last few weeks haven't been a barrel of laughs for me."

"Not for me either. And definitely not for Mary Kate or for her family," Shane immediately retorted.

Jamie looked down at the table and, after a few seconds, continued. "Could I have blocked it out? It's possible, but I really don't think I could have. I know I've had blackouts from drink before, and I certainly had a lot to drink that night. But I've never, ever been violent towards a woman in my life. And to do that to Mary Kate? You know I wouldn't harm a hair on her head. I couldn't. Listen, Shane," Jamie paused, "I truly believe I am not capable of doing that to anybody, let alone Mary Kate. But I've been over it a thousand times in my head, and there's a big gap there. I just can't remember." Jamie's voice was now raised, and he banged his fist against the table.

Shane looked levelly at him. "Which obviously leads to my second question. Why did you tell the cops you did it? Why did you sign a confession?"

To Shane, this was the crux of the issue. Initially, they had heard from the cops that Jamie was claiming amnesia and Shane had struggled to believe that no one would not be able to remember something so terrible, so intense. But then, three days later, the cops came back and said that he had made a full confession.

"Did Jamie say how sorry he was?" Shane had asked the detectives. They replied that he had sort of apologised saying that he was, quote, "sorry for my sins." Cryptic, Shane had thought. He was very confused then. Everything told him that he should hate Jamie for what he did, but something just wasn't right. And now he felt he was about to find out.

86

"Yep. I thought that was gonna be your second question," Jamie replied. He composed himself for a moment.

"Shane, that's a very hard question to answer. All I can say to you at this moment is I had my reasons and—"

"No, Jamie. Not good enough. Not by a long stretch. You swore to me you'd answer truthfully, and now you're giving me some bullshit with 'I have my reasons.'" Shane imitated Jamie's voice nastily. "No. I have to know. I need to know everything."

"It's not that simple," Jamie replied.

"I didn't ask you whether it was simple or not," Shane said. "Just tell me and let me make up my own mind, Jamie."

"Okay, Shane. I'll tell you. But first, you must swear before Almighty God that you will never repeat to a living soul what I'm going to tell you. If I ever choose to tell, it's my business and nobody else's. That's the only condition I have."

"I swear," said Shane immediately, although he didn't attach the same importance to this oath as Jamie did. He had always found Jamie's religious beliefs to be over the top.

Jamie then let out a deep sigh.

"I did it to save Mary Kate," he said.

Shane was totally unprepared for such a statement. He waited for him to continue, but Jamie just stared at him.

"I don't get it. You'll have to explain that to me," Shane said, breaking the silence.

"I don't expect you or anybody else to understand. You know, Shane, I see the world differently than you and other people do. You know I firmly believe that we are only passing through, and our rewards await us in Heaven. You know that?"

"Yes, I do, Jamie," replied Shane.

"Well, the way I saw it at the time was the only person who knows who nearly killed Mary Kate is Mary Kate. The cops were at pains to point out that nobody else could have done it except me, and to be honest, it's very hard to find fault with their arguments. You and I know that Mary Kate wouldn't have answered her door after you left her that night, and I was the only person in the apartment with her. You follow me so far?"

"Go on."

"As I've told you, I can't remember. So, Shane, I prayed. I prayed so hard, prayed like I had never prayed before. But I didn't pray for myself. I prayed that the Lord would spare Mary Kate, and he would save her in the same way he saved Lazarus and brought him back from the dead. And then the Lord answered my prayers."

"Jamie, I'm struggling here big time," Shane interrupted. "You confessed to this terrible crime, even though you don't know whether you're guilty or not because *the Lord told you to do it?*"

"I knew you wouldn't understand, and to be honest, I don't expect you to. The way I saw it then, and the way I see it now is it is a test. I have to place my total trust in Him, and He will save us. Mary Kate will be shown mercy, and she will tell them the truth. She will then tell them who attacked her, and she will clear my name." Jamie's voice had become strangely calm.

"Have you gone mad? Jesus, Jamie, you've totally lost it. Man, you're way out there. You've signed a confession. And now you're going to go back and tell a jury that God made you sign it. I don't know if you're going to end up in Mountjoy prison or Dundrum Mental Institution," Shane shouted at Jamie.

"You're missing the point, Shane. I have told you this and nobody else. I don't intend to tell another soul about this, let alone a jury," Jamie responded.

"What? You can't be serious?"

"I have made my bed, and I have put my complete and utter trust in the Lord. It is in His hands now," Jamie said, casting his eyes towards the heavens.

"Oh, man, this is unbelievable. I don't believe what I'm hearing. Do you know how fucked up your logic is? What if she doesn't recover? What if she dies? Where are you then? If you tell them this after she dies, they'll never believe you. Your only hope is to tell the truth and to tell it now. I'm not sure what difference it will make, but I know for sure it will make no difference if you come out with it—" He was about to finish 'after she dies' but stopped himself.

"No, Shane. That's not going to happen. What will be will be."

"All your clichés are wonderful, Jamie. What will be will be. I've made my bed. It's in His hands now. Blah, blah, blah. But guess what, pal? They won't be worth a damn to you when they send you down for life. Here's another cliché for you—wake up and smell the coffee. Man, you really defy logic!" Shane shouted at him.

"Shane, thank you for what you've done for me. I can't even imagine how hard that was for you, and I really appreciate it. But I am at peace with my decision," replied Jamie calmly and precisely.

Shane was now exhausted. He didn't know how he felt. He was no nearer the truth as to what happened that night, and he had extremely conflicting emotions towards Jamie.

Frustration—absolutely.

Admiration—definitely not.

Respect—NO.

Loyalty—maybe.

He had always known that Jamie was different, but that had made him such a good friend. Jamie had never put himself first and had been very attentive to the needs of others. He looked for the best in people and willingly overlooked their failings.

But now he was testing Shane's patience to the limit. Probably, most of all now, he felt anger—anger towards Jamie for his stupidity. He should have let him rot in prison.

However, it wasn't just anger he felt. Shane wouldn't admit it to himself, and he refused to think about it, but ever since that fateful night, he felt guilt—enormous guilt. He had left her that night and, no matter what anybody said, he was responsible. He wasn't there for her that night when she needed him. He had failed to protect her.

"The truth will out. Is that it, Jamie? I don't think you're telling me the whole story. What state of mind were you in when you 'saw the light'?" Shane asked sarcastically. "Why, if the Lord God Almighty showed you the way, did it take you so long to confess? What really happened in the Garda Station?" Shane then lowered his voice. "Come on, Jamie. It's me, Shane. You know you can tell me everything. You know we don't hold out on each other. Come on, Buddy" he coaxed gently.

"Shane, in order to understand my decision, you must—" Jamie began, but Shane cut across him.

"I don't want to understand your decision. I just want to know what happened. I need answers. Did they beat you up? Is that it, Jamie? Did they beat the confession out of you? Please, tell me," Shane implored once more.

"Please, Shane. It's not relevant how I came to arrive at my decision—"

"So that's a yes."

"It's not relevant," Jamie said decisively.

"It's very relevant to me. Please, just answer yes or no."

Jamie looked at his friend, at his pleading eyes. He had figured that Shane would want to know about his treatment at the hands of the cops. All young men were well aware how the cops went about their business, how heavy-handed they could be. They took no shit from anybody, and you didn't mess with them. A good clip around the ear or a few slaps was the order of the day. But that was normally associated with vandalism or petty crime or acting the maggot.

But beating a confession out of somebody?

Jamie finally answered the question.

"No," he replied.

"No," repeated Shane. "You sure? If the confession was beaten out of you, the judge could set it aside, and the only evidence against you then would be purely circumstantial. Are you absolutely sure? Please, don't lie to me. I believe you when you say you can't remember what happened that night, I really do, but I think you're holding back on me about the cops. Look, Jamie, there's no shame attached to you if you cracked in there. That's what they do, and they're very good at it."

"I'm sure," answered Jamie. He wasn't at all sure, but he had decided at the moment that his deal with God was his only course of action. He would stick with it come what may. Anything else was a distraction.

"God damn you, Jamie," Shane sighed. "All right, that's it then. I was also thinking, Jamie. This is our last time discussing this. Otherwise, it's going to consume us, and you'll drive me nuts. So if there's anything else you want to tell me, anything I should know, now's the time. Well?"

"No. That's it," replied Jamie immediately. In the journey down to Cliften, he had briefly considered telling Shane about his trump card, even if it existed, but he had decided it would form no part of the test that the Lord had set him.

"Well, Jamie, I sincerely hope your God is right because there will be consequences, severe consequences if he lets you down," Shane finished as he handed Jamie a bottle of Smithwicks.

"One other thing. I don't drink anymore," said Jamie.

"Probably a wise decision," replied Shane.

Chapter 16

"WHICH LEFT? MY left or your left? Come on, Deirdre. Help me here. I have a closing to go to later, and I need to get a reply out to that letter today. I already told the client it went out last week."

Tom Dylan was, as usual, in a sweat, rummaging through heaps of paper for a mislaid document. His secretary, Deirdre, calmly walked back into his office and immediately put her hand on the relevant letter.

"Here it is, Tom. I told you, on the left-hand side of the desk near the window, not *on* your desk." She looked around at the files piled high and scattered around his office. Deirdre had long since given up trying to put manners on the office. As soon as she would have it organised, Tom would flip when he couldn't put his hand on something and blame her for messing up his system. Originally, she had thought that it was organised chaos, but she soon realised that it was just chaos—pure bloody chaos.

Deirdre had joined Tom's small legal practice as his legal (and only) secretary over two years ago and was well used to his ways. It still amazed her how he managed to get any work done. The billings were now two months in arrears, and she felt certain she could open any file and find correspondence that remained unanswered. She was easily fifteen years his senior, and had worked in three solicitors' offices before, but never anywhere like this. But she loved it.

Well, more importantly, she loved Tom. He had to be the most disorganised, unreliable solicitor she had ever met. But he was also the kindest, most charismatic, caring individual she had ever known. When someone would come to the office, in the depths of some seemingly intractable problem, Tom's soothing voice put them at ease and took their troubles away. He seemed to hypnotise them. Nothing was ever a problem to him, and the poor man was a sucker for a hard luck story. He hadn't the heart to charge properly and often, ended up doing the work for free or at a ridiculously low rate. As a result, many sad cases in Dublin ended up on Tom's desk. He was working flat out, but making very little money.

Tom read the letter that Deirdre had handed him and dictated a response.

"There. That will keep them off my back for a while. This afternoon, Deirdre, we need to do some more work on the Jamie Ryan case. I think we're coming very near to a trial date," he said to her. "I want to look at those notes again. I just can't figure them out."

It was now almost eighteen months since Mary Kate was attacked. The poor girl was alive, technically speaking. She was still in a coma. The medical people were sure it was the machines prolonging her life. They suggested, on more than one occasion, that it would be best for everybody if they were switched off and allow nature to take its course. However, her mother wouldn't hear of it.

The family had maintained a twenty-four-hour bedside vigil for the first three months. However, as time marched on, jobs had to be held down, and people slowly started to return to their normal lives—not that anything felt normal anymore, after what had happened. Mary Kate's only daily visitor was her loving mother, who still sat and spoke to her for the best part of every day. The others, including her father, were now occasional visitors. It was not that they had stopped caring—they cared and loved too much. They had given up hope and could no longer endure the pain of seeing Mary Kate lying there lifeless. She still looked so beautiful and at peace. It was as if she were just sleeping. But, in their eyes, she was dead. But not in the eyes of her mother. Jane Quinn would never give up on her daughter.

"Yes. I heard that the prosecution reckon they'll be ready in about five or six weeks and might apply for a trial date next week," Deirdre said.

Both Tom and Deirdre were extremely anxious about the case. It was Tom's only criminal case (drunk driving and shoplifting didn't count in his eyes), and it was so serious and so high profile, it overwhelmed him. Every time he met Jamie, he pleaded with him to be excused from the case. He wanted to get Jamie better representation, somebody who knew what they were doing— someone who, at the very least, knew their way around criminal law. One of the country's top criminal lawyers, Wesley Kelly, had even rung Tom and offered to take over the case. But Jamie wouldn't hear of it. "You're my man, Tom," he would say with a smile. "I have faith in you." Little did Tom know Jamie couldn't care less.

The first note had arrived about three weeks ago. It simply read: JAMIE RYAN COULDN'T HAVE DONE IT. ASK HIM.

Tom was taken aback and went straight to the wastepaper basket to retrieve the envelope it had arrived in. There was no stamp, no postmark, so it must have been hand delivered.

The notepaper and the envelope were of good quality, and his name and the cryptic message was written in small, neat print. The size of the notepaper was unusual. It was the width of a standard A4 sheet, but only about three-quarters of its length.

He had called Deirdre into his office.

"What do you think of that?" he asked, showing Deirdre the note.

"Mmmm," she muttered. "Not much, actually. What am I meant to think of a note that doesn't even have a signature? I'd say it's some crank or nutter," she said over her shoulder, returning to her office.

"But what if it's genuine?" Tom stammered. "Do you think he could be innocent?"

"It doesn't matter a hoot whether he's innocent or not. What does matter is whether they have enough evidence to convict. That's all there is to it. Whether he's innocent or not doesn't come into it," Deirdre retorted. She was convinced Tom should try to persuade the judge to release him from the case even if Jamie wouldn't. He was totally out of his depth.

"Hold on, Deirdre. Sit down and listen. Let me think." Tom rubbed his face with both hands.

Deirdre plonked herself down on the chair, not attempting to disguise the fact that she had better things to do and considered this a waste of time.

"Okay. You could be right. It could be a hoax, some sicko getting his kicks. But, if it's for real, it seems to be saying that Jamie himself knows he didn't do it." He picked up the note again and read it aloud.

JAMIE RYAN COULDN'T HAVE DONE IT. ASK HIM.

"Ask him? If Jamie knows he couldn't have done it, why would he have signed the confession? And why couldn't he have done it? Puzzling," Tom finished, still very deep in thought.

"As I said, some nutter—" began Deirdre, but Tom jumped up and interrupted

"I think I have it. Bear with me. Maybe Jamie couldn't have done it because he wasn't there. Maybe he was with whoever wrote the note. That person is his alibi, and there is some reason why Jamie won't reveal where he was and who he was with ..." Tom stopped. "Does that make sense to you?"

"Absolutely not, Tom. For two reasons. One, it totally contradicts the evidence in the case. Remember he was found lying on the floor in her locked apartment. And two, he signed a confession and has never once said that he wasn't there. I think Jamie realises the charges he faces, even if she doesn't die, are very serious. Do you not think that if he had an alibi, it would have been the first thing he would have said?"

"He's a funny fish, though," replied Tom.

"Not that funny. Nobody's that funny." What a waste of time, thought Deirdre as she turned and went back to her office.

"One last thing I just thought of," Tom shouted after her. "What if the note is from the real assailant?"

"Well, Tom, you know what you have to do then," Deirdre responded.

"What's that?"

Deirdre's patience was really growing thin now.

"As the note says—ask him."

Chapter 17

"WHAT YOU KNOW you can't tell. You can't tell a soul. Remember, we discussed this. I needn't remind you of the consequences if you open your mouth. Remember your oath and SHUT THE FUCK UP. Okay?" Jamie roared as he slammed down the phone, not giving any opportunity for a response.

A few hours earlier, Jamie had been in Tom's office. They were discussing the procedural aspects of the impending trial when Tom suddenly handed him the note and sat back to observe his reaction. He was startled to see Jamie's face contort suddenly with anger. Christ, this note *did* mean something.

"You know what, Jamie, I wasn't sure about this note, but now I know that this note is genuine. What does it mean by you couldn't have done it? Tell me. Who are you trying to protect, and from what?"

Jamie had to think fast.

He muttered something, hoping to keep Tom at bay.

"No, Tom. I'm just intrigued by this note. I can't make sense of it. When did you receive it again?" Jamie replied, trying to buy some time. He was like a rabbit caught in the headlights—he couldn't work out his next move.

He was so tempted to grasp the opportunity that the note presented, to end the madness. But he needed time to think, time to figure out what was best. He couldn't just think of himself—he had to think of Mary Kate and whether God would let her live or not. Maybe this was part of God's test, or maybe this was God reaching out to him to save him. But he didn't know. He needed time to think, to pray for guidance. At the moment, though, he had to stay focused and stonewall Tom.

"Jamie, please stop lying to me. I can tell by your reaction that you know exactly what the note is all about. I bet you that you even know who wrote it. Jamie, somebody is trying to help you here. Please, tell me exactly what happened that night. Why is he, or maybe she, saying you couldn't have done it?" Tom pleaded with him but could tell he was getting nowhere. Jamie just sat there, his hands now tucked under his legs, looking down at the floor.

Jamie felt as if he was back in the Garda station.

"Tom, the facts speak for themselves. I was found lying next to her in a locked apartment. Nobody else was there. I can't fathom why somebody would write such a note. Do you think it's genuine?" Jamie knew there was only one person who could have written that note, but now was not the time to tell.

"Fine, Jamie. Have it your way. I recognise that tone of voice and your defensive body language. You've shut down. You're not going to let anyone help you. I really don't understand you," Tom replied in exasperation.

Actually, at this stage, Tom was beginning to understand Jamie. Whatever had happened or whatever Jamie knew, Jamie wasn't going to divulge, and the harder people pushed, the more he retreated. But what the hell had happened that night? Who was he protecting and, more importantly, why?

Chapter 18

"THE TRIAL DATE has been set for the third of October," Deidre announced to Tom as he returned from his closing. "And what's more, they say they have uncovered new evidence, which further proves that young Mr. Ryan is guilty."

"What new evidence could there be? Sure, it's nearly twenty months since the crime," replied Tom.

"Wouldn't say, but they're couriering it over now."

Tom slumped into his chair. The third of October—that was only two weeks away! The reality of an actual trial date frightened the life out of him. He had hoped that it would never come to this, that he would have managed to extricate himself from the case before now. There was still no swaying Jamie. Tom had even broken all rules and gone behind Jamie's back and had spoken to Shane.

"Look, Shane, you and I know I'm not the right man for the job. As a matter of fact, Jamie knows that as well." He had spoken frankly to Shane one afternoon when they were alone.

Much to his father's chagrin, since Jamie was granted bail, Jamie and Shane had grown inseparable. They had remained holed up together in their small Cliften cottage all this time. Shane had made tremendous sacrifices for Jamie. His relationship with his family was hanging by a thread, and his beautiful girlfriend had broken up with him. He had deferred his medical studies (some would say he had dropped out.) As the case got closer to trial, he travelled with Jamie to his meetings with Tom, and lately, at Jamie's insistence, he attended their meetings—Jamie said he was making Shane part of his legal team. Tom wasn't sure whether this was permitted or not, but that's the way it was.

"That's Jamie's call, Tom. You know that," Shane had replied.

"But surely, you can talk sense into him. There's no point him going into court with one hand tied behind his back. At least, let me talk to Wesley Kelly and have him guide me. Please, Shane, talk to him," Tom pleaded.

"It will do no good, Tom. For right or wrong, his mind is set. Let it be," Shane had replied.

Tom was now pacing the room, anxiously waiting for the new evidence to arrive. He would definitely be phoning Wesley Kelly about this. I mean, surely they couldn't introduce new evidence at this point? What was new about it? How long have they had it? What—

"Tom, will you please sit down before you drive me demented. All will be revealed shortly," Deirdre shouted at him, using her schoolteacher tone again. One of these days, he must have a word with her about that. After all, he was the boss. But he knew she always meant well and had his best interests at heart.

At last, the courier arrived, and Tom ripped open the small envelope.

"It's an affidavit from a Siobhan Williams, fairly short affidavit actually, only about seven pages. Is this the new evidence?" he said, more of a statement rather than a question.

"Well, you won't know until you read it," Deirdre replied. Sometimes, he really tried her patience.

"Oh, yeah, right so," and then disappeared into his office.

102

Deirdre hovered outside for what seemed like an eternity, waiting for his inevitable call. At last, it came.

"Deirdre, come in here quickly. I need your help," he hollered.

"We must send a telegram immediately to Jamie. I have to meet him as a matter of great urgency," he blustered as he wiped the sweat from his brow. "This girl's testimony is explosive."

Deirdre looked at him evenly.

"Right away, Deirdre. We've no time to waste. I absolutely must speak to him."

"What was in the affidavit, Tom? Who is Siobhan Williams?" she asked him calmly.

"Here it is. Read it for yourself. Oh, Deirdre, will you also get me Wesley Kelly on the phone?" he said as he raced to the toilet. The poor man was in an awful state.

Twenty minutes later, Deirdre had neither sent a telegram to Jamie nor attempted to get Wesley Kelly on the phone. She had high regard for Mr. Kelly as a criminal lawyer but had very little time for him as a person. Such an obnoxious, condescending man.

"Here, I've made you a nice cup of tea."

"Never mind that. Did you get Wesley Kelly? What am I going to do? This will bury him. How do I deal with it? How?"

"You don't."

"What? Come on, Deirdre. You've read what this Siobhan Williams has to say. After her evidence, the jury will be baying for his blood. They'll have a field day with her in the witness box."

"She'll never see the witness box," she replied smugly.

Sometimes she could really get under his skin.

"I don't follow," he finally said.

As far as he was concerned, Siobhan Williams was the final nail in the coffin of Jamie Ryan. At best, he had a very weak defence, the facts of the case spoke for themselves, and Jamie had also signed a confession that he had never once retracted, but now, with her testimony, the case was a slam-dunk.

"Tom," pausing, she took a deep breath, "I firmly believe that her statement is inadmissible in court as it would be very prejudicial to the case. A judge will never let the jury see her affidavit, let alone allow her to take the stand. The court is only concerned—and furthermore, can only concern itself—with the events of that night. The prosecution must prove, beyond a reasonable doubt that Jamie Ryan attempted to murder—the first charge—and raped—the second charge, Mary Kate Quinn."

Deirdre chose her words very carefully and spoke slowly.

She paused briefly to allow Tom take in everything she had said and then continued.

"Therefore, any events that happened prior to that particular night are irrelevant and totally inadmissible in court. Siobhan Williams' evidence against Jamie would be highly prejudicial. It will most certainly not be allowed."

"Surely, Deirdre, that can't be correct! Her evidence shows what he is capable of. If it's inadmissible, as you say, then please answer me this. Why are they introducing it into evidence? They obviously believe that she will be allowed to testify."

"I very much doubt it."

"I don't follow."

"Obviously, Tom, the prosecution team is testing you. They're seeing how much they can get away with, how up to speed you are. And frankly, Tom, I'm very worried for you. I don't mean to be insolent, but a first-year law student would know that Siobhan Williams will never be heard. Her evidence has nothing to do with the case."

"But it shows that he has previous?" Poor Tom was now bewildered.

"If he is found guilty, I think, though I'm not sure, it can be brought up regarding sentencing. Let me give you an example." She really needed him to understand. "Say if you had a guy who had served his time for murder and then kills another person after he was released, the jury wouldn't be allowed to know anything about the previous conviction. The trial could only hear the evidence in relation to the murder that he stands accused of," Deirdre explained.

"Okay, I get the point, although it seems ridiculous to me."

"For right or wrong, it's our legal system," Deirdre replied.

"It kind of proves he did it, though. You just wouldn't think he had it in him. I mean, he comes across as—"

"Tom, stop it right now." Deirdre was cross, and the schoolteacher's voice was back again. "You have to stop thinking like that. It doesn't matter whether he did it or not. What matters is what the evidence says. That's all. And your legal obligation is to provide him with the best defence possible. You cannot let your own personal opinions come into play."

"Yes, Deirdre, I know. But it baffles me. Here you have an ex-girlfriend of Jamie Ryan, who says that he attempted to rape her one night, and she thought he was going to kill her. Yet it has no bearing on his case. Unbelievable."

Chapter 19

THE TRIAL WAS less than a week away. Joe Quinn sat at the end of Mary Kate's hospital bed, staring out the window. He knew what had to be said, but he kept postponing the inevitable. But now, he was rapidly running out of time.

He looked at Mary Kate to help him summon up the courage to speak. It was now or never.

"Jane, love, I really think it's time we let her go."

Joe had approached the subject on numerous occasions, but this was the first time he had been so forthright about it. There was no maybes, no ifs, no 'it might be for the best.' However, the words 'I think' had crept in, and he was annoyed with himself about that. He didn't want to show any sign of weakness.

"No. I won't hear of it. I'm not deserting her. I'm not giving up on her," Jane replied, as he expected she would.

But this time, it was all or nothing for Joe. He just hoped he had the guts to follow through. It had the potential to destroy her, but he couldn't carry on like this. The family couldn't.

"Jane, darling, we all loved Mary Kate."

She immediately shot him daggers and interrupted.

"Loved? Don't you dare ever talk about her in the past tense."

"I will," he said brazenly. He had deliberately chosen to speak about her in the past tense, knowing full well it would provoke this reaction from his wife.

"Jane, love, please listen to me. That's not Mary Kate lying in that bed. It may be her flesh and bones, but it's not our baby in that bed." The tears started to roll down his cheeks.

"Her spirit left a long time ago. You've heard what the doctors said, they said that—"

"No. I'm not ready for this. Please, Joe, leave it be."

"I can't leave it, Jane. It's not about what you want. Please stop thinking about yourself and think of others, and what they need."

"But I am, Joe," she pleaded. "I'm thinking of Mary Kate."

"No, you're not." He knew he had to carry on, but he wasn't sure if he had the strength. His heart was close to breaking as he saw the utter devastation etched all over his wife's face.

"You're thinking of yourself. You can't bear to lose her. But what about Mary Kate? You're keeping her here, in limbo. The doctors have said that, as far as they know, there's no brain activity. It's only the machines prolonging her life if you could call it a life."

"No, Joe, that's not true. You'll see, Joe. She'll wake up. She will. One day. You'll see. Please don't give up on her, Joe. Please don't make me do this," Jane was sobbing uncontrollably.

Enough of this. He couldn't carry on. He was never any good at playing the tough guy and immediately rushed over to comfort his wife.

"Oh, Jane, Jane, I'm so sorry. I know how hard this is on you," he cried as he embraced her.

Patrick peered in through the glass panel of the door and waited for his parents to end their embrace. He had hoped it wouldn't come to this but guessed all along that it would. His father was no James Dean.

Deep breath.

He walked into the room.

"Mam, what would Mary Kate do if she were standing here?"

"Patrick, love?"

"Do you think this is what she would want? To be kept alive by a bunch of machines, not capable of doing anything for herself? And for how long? How much longer? Another month, two months, two years? Well?"

"But, Patrick…"

"No, Mam. We need to have closure, and we have to face facts. Mary Kate is clinically dead and keeping her alive like this is against everything Mary Kate stood for. She was so full of life, Mam. Please, she wouldn't thank you for this. You have to let her go."

"But I love her so much."

"We all do. You don't have a monopoly on that. But this is destroying what we have left as a family. You have to come back to us, Mam, and let her go. I can't take it anymore. Dad can't take it anymore. It's like when Jamie took Mary Kate from us, he took you, too."

Patrick also had an ulterior motive, one that he most definitely wasn't going to discuss with his mother. It was actually his grandfather, the politician, who had raised it with him.

"You know, the way things are, the little bastard will get away with murder, literally," his grandfather had said.

"What do you mean?" Patrick had replied.

"Well, as things stand, Mary Kate is alive, as least technically speaking. Therefore, he can't be tried for murder, only for attempted murder. My contacts in the judiciary inform me that it's a more difficult prosecution. Juries tend to err on the side of caution. They tend to be more sympathetic to the dead, being more inclined to give the deceased justice. Plus it would mean a substantially longer prison sentence."

Patrick knew he was being played by his grandfather, but, more than anything else, he craved justice for Mary Kate. He had never thought it possible to feel such hatred for a person.

Nothing was going to stop him from saying what had to be said.

"Mam, what was her favourite saying?"

"That's not relevant here," she said deliberately avoiding eye contact with him.

"It most certainly is. Tell me, Mam. Say the words."

Jane Quinn lowered her head and whispered, "What will be will be."

"Then do right by her and respect her. End this madness now, for all our sakes."

Jane stood up and walked over to face her son, her accuser.

"And what would you have me do?"—her face in his face—"I can't kill my own daughter."

"You're not killing her, Mam. Jamie already did that. All you're doing is setting her free. Please, Mam."

"I can't."

"You have to. Mam, just answer me one question, and then I'll shut up. Okay? If that were me lying there and Mary Kate was standing here where I am now, what would she do? Would she set me free? Would she face up to reality? This has already destroyed one life. Let it not destroy anymore."

Jane didn't answer, and Patrick didn't push it any further. She looked him in the eye for a few moments and then moved over to Mary Kate's bed, lay down beside her and began gently stroking her daughter's face.

Chapter 20

TWO DAYS HAD passed since Joe and Patrick had confronted Jane. At first, she carried on as before and deliberately refused to even think about what they had said to her.

But Patrick's words kept invading her thoughts. "What would Mary Kate do?"

She tried to ignore the question, but it dominated her mind, screaming at her to be answered. It now pursued her relentlessly. She wouldn't answer because she knew the answer.

She was so tired. All she wanted was peace. How did it come to this?

As a nurse, she had dealt with many demented souls and had never been able to understand how life could become unbearable.

She thought about her previous life, how happy and carefree it was. She yearned for those times again.

She had always thought suicide was the coward's way out but now, as she held the bottle of tablets in her hand, it felt like the perfect solution.

Chapter 21

FATHER WALSH LED the family in prayer as they gathered around her bedside. Her favourite song, 'Let It Be', was playing in the background. They were trying to remain positive, but it was utterly futile.

Jane had finally consented to turn off the machines. Yesterday, she had lain on her bed with a bottle of pills in hand staring into the abyss. But something was holding her back. She felt she couldn't face her altered life, life without Mary Kate. She also realised that her marriage was hanging by a thread. She had become totally consumed with her daughter and had neglected everybody else. But something else that Patrick had said struck a chord.

"This has already destroyed one life. Let it not destroy anymore."

She was nobody's fool, but sometimes, you have to think of yourself. She wasn't sure if she could face this world anymore.

The doorbell rang.

She wouldn't answer it.

The doorbell rang again.

My God, even in my hour of need, you won't give me peace.

She answered it. It was Father Walsh.

As soon as she saw him, she let loose. All her pent-up grief and anger came flooding out. She pounded on his chest, screeching.

"I've always lived by the rules, always been a good Catholic. Why has He done this to us? Why did He let it happen?" she screamed.

He stood there silent, knowing no words would make sense at this time. He was a very good priest, but even he found it extremely difficult at times to understand the workings of his Master.

She cursed Jamie Ryan, damned his soul to Hell, and said that she would NEVER EVER forgive him. He listened. She stopped hitting him, and he held her in his arms.

Eventually, after a few minutes, the tears stopped, and he released her. She took one step back from him and whispered, "I have to let her go, set her free. That's what she would want, isn't it, Father?"

"Yes, my child."

The medics had said that once they turned off the ventilator, she would not be able to breathe by herself. It would only be a matter of minutes before she passed away. Father Walsh had finished his work and was silent. They had formed a human chain around her holding each other tightly. There was now no going back. Joe lifted his head and gave the order.

"Do it."

It was done.

The grief in the room was palpable. Jane immediately broke the chain and lay down beside her daughter, stroking her hair and face as she had done for the previous twenty months.

Mary Kate started to breathe by herself.

Chapter 22

THE DAY OF the trial had finally arrived. Both the prosecution and the defence had briefly considered seeking an adjournment in light of Mary Kate's ability to breathe unaided. But that was all she had done. She had shown no further signs of any recovery. Furthermore, the medics had dismissed any notion that she would come out of her coma and reveal her secret.

"We must remember that breathing is an involuntary action. For example, we all know that we continue breathing even when we are asleep. It doesn't necessarily follow that, because she can breathe by herself, she will make any more progress," Dr. Kennedy had informed the family.

"But this is totally unexpected. You said she wouldn't be able to breathe by herself, that she would pass away peacefully. Surely this is a good sign. It has to be a positive development," Joe quizzed.

"I really don't want to give you false hope. I'll repeat all the tests again to confirm that there is no brain activity."

"How can she be breathing by herself if there is no brain activity?" Joe persisted.

"It is most unusual. To be honest, I just don't understand it,"

Dr. Kennedy replied.

But Jamie Ryan did. He understood it completely. The timing was no coincidence. He had passed the test, and the Lord would now save him and spare Mary Kate. This was the miracle he had prayed so hard for. Jamie Ryan was euphoric.

Tom and Shane had tried to impress on him that, at this moment in time, it didn't change anything. There was absolutely no guarantee whatsoever that she would regain consciousness. In fact, according to all professional opinion, the opposite was much more likely. But nothing could convince Jamie otherwise. His nightmare was nearing an end.

They had anticipated a large crowd in court, and they weren't wrong. Jamie did his best to focus and to follow Tom's instructions. Tom had told them that the start of the trial would be quite explosive. The prosecution would outline all the charges against him and do their utmost to portray him as an evil, callous rapist.

"Remember, Jamie, it's all about the jury. You only get one chance to make a first impression, and it is absolutely critical. The jury must like you, they must empathise with you. You must remain calm and composed at all times. Got it?" Tom had lectured him.

However, Jamie remaining calm was the least of Tom's worries at this particular time. Tom was expecting to be nervous, but this was ridiculous. He anticipated the adrenalin would kick in, but it was now overpowering him. He genuinely felt he could not control his bodily functions. He had prepared as well as he could for this day, but he knew he was completely out of his depth. He did not belong in this courtroom. He had nearly vomited when he saw the size of the prosecution team. In his mind, they were staring and sneering at him and could see the sheer panic written all over his face. Soon, he would be exposed as a fraud. He wanted to run. No matter how often he wiped his brow, the sweat kept dripping.

"Relax, Tom. Everything will work out," Jamie said as he

gently patted him on his arm. Tom hadn't realised that he was physically shaking. "You've prepared well and done your best. It's in God's hands now."

Patronising little fuck, Tom thought. *Come on, Tom. Pull yourself together, man. It's now or never,* he told himself sternly.

"No, Jamie. It's in our hands now. Nobody else's. Please remember that. There ain't no God in this courtroom." The authority in Tom's voice even surprised himself. He looked down and studied his notes one more time. The trial would commence in less than ten minutes.

Seeing that Tom was engrossed in his notes yet again, Jamie leaned back and spoke briefly to Shane, who was sitting behind him. It was only small talk and Jamie only half listened to Shane, but it was his opportunity to scan the courtroom and see who was there. Or, more importantly to Jamie, to see who wasn't there. As expected, his mother was sitting at the back of the court, but there was no sign of his father. Or his two older brothers for that matter. Even though his mother had warned him they wouldn't be there, he still hoped they would be.

It hurt Jamie deeply, but he had decided that, after Mary Kate had exonerated him, he would be very magnanimous. He'd had the conversation many times already in his mind:

"Oh, son, I'm so sorry. I should never have deserted you like that. I should never have doubted you. I'm such a coward. Can you ever forgive me?"

"Dad, don't be so hard on yourself. You'll always be my father. Of course, I forgive you." And then his father would hug him fiercely, and Jamie would comfort him as he wept.

But Jamie found it hard to suppress the anger and disappointment he felt towards his father. He could see it from his father's point of view, what with the confession the overwhelming circumstantial evidence, but, damn it, he was still his son, after all.

Jamie did not dare look at the other side of the courtroom. There were a lot of people there who had waited a long time for this day. Among the crowd, Patrick sat staring, not at Jamie, but at his cousin Shane. In his eyes, Shane had utterly deserted Mary Kate. He had done so that night, leaving her alone with that bastard in the apartment. And now he was deserting her again, sitting, and chatting away with her murderer. He was nearly as guilty as Jamie.

Shane's father sat beside Patrick, but he just looked straight ahead. He could not bring himself to look at his son. Shane had brought such shame on the family.

"Jamie," Tom tapped his arm. "You know we spoke at length previously about the circumstances of your confession. Are you one hundred percent sure that everything occurred in the Garda station the way they said it did?"

"We've been through this before, Tom. If that's how the guards said it happened, well then, that's how it happened."

He knew Jamie was lying, but he couldn't break him. Jamie had actually burst out laughing when they had reviewed the custody sergeants' records in relation to his detention.

"Sure it was like staying in a four-star hotel, all those fine meals and rest periods I had." Jamie had scoffed when he read them.

But when Tom had pushed him hard on that point, "If there is a procedural deficiency"—a phrase Tom had picked up from Wesley Kelly—"the confession could be deemed inadmissible, and it's the main evidence against you."

Jamie had asked him one question. "The custody sergeant, he wasn't either of the guards who interviewed me, correct?"

Tom knew what he meant. If there was a cover-up, they were all in it together. Tom would have liked an opportunity to put the guards in the witness box, but Jamie was having none of it.

"Who do you think they're going to believe?" was Jamie's final statement on the matter.

The moment had now arrived.

"All rise. The Right Honourable Judge Maura Walsh presiding."

"In thee, O Lord, I put my trust," Jamie whispered.

Tom looked over at him just as the door of the courtroom flung open with a loud thud. A rather large man, obviously out of breath from running, approached the leading prosecutor and handed him a note.

"This had better be imperative for anybody to disrupt my court in such a fashion," the judge bellowed.

"My apologies to the court, Your Honour, but there has been a significant development in this case. I would be extremely grateful if the Court could grant a short recess at this time. The key witness for the prosecution, Mary Kate Quinn, has just spoken."

Chapter 23

JAMIE, SHANE, AND Tom sat in Tom's office waiting for a call. Time seemed to have stopped. The waiting was killing them. They sat in silence, deep in their own thoughts. All their lives had been dramatically affected by this case.

Shane finally broke the silence.

"I can't take it anymore. I want to go over and see her, talk to her. After all, she is still my cousin."

"No, Shane," Tom said. "We had better wait. We really don't know what's going on. We don't know if she's sitting up in bed, eating toast and chatting away, or if she uttered something that sounded like a word as the nurses turned her. Remember, they only asked for a short recess rather than the trial to be adjourned. If she had…"

"Ifs and buts," Jamie jumped in.

"Look, I'm just saying. She has been in a coma for a long time. Maybe she's singing away like a canary or maybe she can't remember anything. Maybe, at this moment in time, she doesn't even know her own name," Tom continued. "Hopefully, we will all be a lot wiser at two o'clock."

Shane looked at Jamie.

"Have you thought of the other possibility?" he said.

"Yes."

There was nothing further said. Both men understood each other. What if she had woken up, and Jamie had actually done it?

"Jamie, we have to stay focused," said Tom, deliberately swaying the conversation back to the here and now. "We have to face the real prospect that this will have no bearing on the trial. Even if there is no permanent brain damage to Mary Kate, which is extremely unlikely given the length of time she's been in a coma, and she's able to talk, she may never be able to recall the events of that night. We have to prepare ourselves for that." The more Tom thought about it, the more he felt this would turn out to be nothing more than a distraction, and the trial would continue at two o'clock.

Jamie nodded, but he was only giving him lip service. He knew that the nightmare was coming to an end. He indulged himself, allowing his mind to drift to thoughts of his former life surrounded by his family and friends. He could feel his father's embrace and could smell his scent.

By one-forty p.m., they hadn't received a call and made their way back to the court. However, Jamie remained in high spirits. Tom was becoming seriously worried about him. He was sure this would turn out to be a red herring. At best, he believed the trial might be postponed for a few weeks, or months, maybe, to fully assess Mary Kate's medical condition. He just couldn't fathom how somebody who was clinically dead could now be talking.

The court was not as packed this time around. None of Mary Kate's family was there. Presumably still at the hospital, Tom thought. But he was baffled when the court rose, and the prosecution team wasn't there either. However, just as the judge was about to let loose about the disrespect being shown to her court, the lead prosecutor appeared.

"My sincere apologies to the court. I beg Your Honour's forgiveness. However, as I said earlier, there has been a major development in this case. I beg the court's indulgence, but we respectfully request permission to amend the charges."

Jamie looked at Tom, who hadn't a clue what was going on. He didn't know whether he should object or not. He was just about to stand to object when the prosecutor continued.

"We wish to drop the charge of attempted murder—"

"YES!" Jamie roared as he jumped to his feet and punched the air—test finally passed, Mary Kate spared.

"—and replace it with the charge of murder."

Jamie Ryan collapsed to the floor.

Chapter 24

THE JUDGE REQUESTED medical attention for Jamie after he collapsed, but it wasn't necessary. By the time the paramedics arrived, he was back on his feet. Legal argument then ensued as to whether the jury should be discharged and a new trial ordered. The judge was of the view that a new trial wasn't necessary and that there was no need for a new jury. Tom had argued forcefully that a new trial was required but, failing that, he requested an adjournment of at least six months, given the severity of the new charge. The judge, after warning Tom that he was in danger of contempt of court if he continued, eventually conceded to an adjournment for four weeks, two weeks more than the prosecution wanted.

After the court had emptied, the full realisation that Mary Kate was dead hit Jamie and Shane. The two young men were overcome with grief, and both wept openly and uncontrollably. However, Jamie and Shane seemed absorbed in their own angst and made no attempt to comfort each other. Tom proceeded to pack up his papers and said nothing. What was there to say? The atmosphere was so emotionally charged that Tom was struggling himself. Even though he had never met Mary Kate, he felt he had known her all his life.

Eventually, Jamie spoke.

"I'd like to say a prayer for her. Will you please join me?"

"Oh, fuck off, will you?" Shane snapped. "You and your fucking God. Don't you think the two of ye have done enough damage already?"

There was no further conversation, and the tears had now stopped, but Tom could still sense Shane's anger. He was like a tightly wound coil ready to snap. Tom tried to imagine how Shane must be feeling right now. He had sacrificed so much for Jamie. He even gave up his medical studies that he had worked so hard for. He had been ostracised by his family, and now this—losing Mary Kate. Tom knew that Mary Kate was like a younger sister to Shane. He had every right to be upset and angry.

"I'm sorry, Jamie. I shouldn't have snapped. Come on. Let's get out of here, go back to Clifden." Shane rose to his feet.

A remarkable young man, thought Tom.

"Shane, could I have a word with you in private, please?" his father approached them, his eyes also red from crying.

"Okay, Dad, sure." He turned to Jamie and Tom. "Don't worry. I'll be right back."

They walked down the corridor of the courthouse in silence as Tim looked for a suitable place to be able to have a private conversation. Shane had spoken to his father on only a handful of occasions since he posted bail for Jamie, the last time being Christmas Day when he rang his family from the phone booth in Clifden. The conversation had been civil and guarded.

Tim directed him outside and stopped at the bicycle shed. He turned to face his son, immediately grabbing and hugging him tightly.

"Oh, Shane, I've missed you so much. I always knew she'd die, but now that she's finally gone, it really hits you. The scene over at the hospital is just horrible. The Quinns are all devastated."

"I just can't believe she's gone," replied Shane as he started to cry again.

"I know, I know," Tim said, and his tears flowed again.

"I'm so sorry, Dad."

They held each other tightly for several minutes, neither of them prepared to let go. The last twenty months or so had taken a terrible toll on everybody.

"Come on home, Shane. Please. It's all over now. We need you at home. Your mother... I miss you terribly. You did what you felt you had to do, but it's over now. Come home now, son," Tim begged.

"No, Dad. Not yet."

"Please, Shane. It's so hard without you around. Your family needs you now more than ever." He paused. "More than Jamie does."

"I'm sorry, Dad. I really wish I could, but I just can't. I have unfinished business with Jamie."

"You heard that she spoke before she died?"

"Yes, Dad, but all I heard was what was said in court."

"She as good as said that Jamie did it."

"What do you mean?"

"Just before she died, Mary Kate jolted in the bed and whispered, "Jamie. Jamie. NO."

Chapter 25

SHANE AND JAMIE again sat facing each other across the kitchen table in their remote cottage in Clifden. Shane had insisted on making a nice cup of tea as they both struggled to take in the events of the day. Shane pulled down one cup, went to the sink, and poured a cup of tea for Jamie.

"One cup. You're not having one yourself?"

"No thanks," Shane replied as he pulled a bottle of Jameson from the press. "I'm going to have something stronger." He proceeded to pour himself a very large glass of whiskey. Jamie still hadn't had a drink since that night. He was sorely tempted to join his friend, but he hadn't been offered. *Perhaps it's for the best,* he thought.

The journey down had been in absolute silence. Shane had switched off the radio before they even left Dublin such was the level of coverage about the death of Mary Kate and the murder charge.

Jamie sipped his tea slowly and tried to read his friend. He had never seen him like this, sensing his anger, but Jamie was at a loss as to what to do or say. To the outside world, her death probably didn't change anything. After all, she had been in a coma for so long and was expected to die. But to Jamie, it changed everything. It rocked him to the core. His God had now well and truly deserted him, leaving him alone to face the wolves. He had never felt such betrayal, such loneliness. His plan hadn't worked—he hadn't been able to save Mary Kate.

But now it was time to save himself. It was time to tell.

However, Jamie felt very tired and was finding it hard to concentrate. He looked across at Shane. Maybe it was his imagination, but Shane seemed to be looking at him in the most peculiar way. A look he had never seen before. It frightened him. He wondered how Shane would react to what he was about to tell him.

Perhaps he should have confided in him at the start, but he was convinced that the course of action he took was the only way of saving Mary Kate. How wrong he had been.

He began to talk, but he was totally exhausted. *I'll tell him in the morning. I'm just so tired.* The next second, his head hit the table.

"Come on. Time to wake up," Shane said. Jamie didn't know how long he had been asleep. He could hear Shane but was finding it very hard to focus. The punch helped him focus very quickly, and he was fully alert after the second punch. Fear gripped him instantly when he opened his eyes.

Jamie tried to move but couldn't. Both his arms and legs were tied very tightly to the kitchen chair. But there was something else. Something very wrong. He was soaked through. He felt extremely groggy and was very confused. And what was that smell?

It was then the enormity of the situation dawned on him.

Jamie Ryan sat tied to the chair doused in petrol. Shane Bradley stood over him, a hunter's knife in one hand and a lighter in the other.

"Enjoy your sleep?" Shane asked. From his limited time studying medicine, he knew exactly what drug and what quantity to put in his tea.

"But Shane—"

"Shh, now, Jamie. I'm in charge. For once, let me do the talking. You see, I know you had your deal with your god, but he fairly fucked you over, didn't he? And me included, for that matter. So yesterday, I made a deal with the Devil." He sighed.

Jamie perceived the sigh as a sign of weakness.

"Shane, this isn't you. This is madness."

Shane towered over him and kicked him on the side of the head, knocking him and the chair over like a skittle in a bowling alley. He dragged him up by the hair and put the chair back in its position.

"This is madness, Jamie, you think? What's madness is that I believed you. I trusted you. I stood by you, and for what? For what, Jamie? For nothing." Shane regained his composure. "Ground rules: I do the talking. You just answer the questions. It's very simple. You tell the truth, you live. You lie, you die. Comprehend?"

He lit the lighter but held it away from the petrol. Jamie was terrified the fumes would set him alight.

"Okay, Shane. I'll tell you the truth. I'll come clean. I'll tell you everything."

Shane smiled. "You've been a bold boy, Jamie. You held out on me, didn't you? The only thing I asked of you was the truth. That was the only thing. There's more to this than 'I can't remember.' Everything I did for you, everything I've been through and you FUCKING WELL held out on me. You swore to me. I thought that meant everything to you. I thought that's who you were. Christ, man. Wasn't I the fool?"

Shane flicked off the lighter and carefully put it on the table.

"And now you're going to tell me everything, eh?"

"Yes, Shane. I will I will."

"Well, Jamie, it's too late. I know all about Siobhan Williams. You don't get the privilege of a last confession. Your sins are going with you when you meet your Maker. No deathbed

131

confession for you."

Shane yanked Jamie back by the hair and slit his throat from ear to ear. A river of blood splashed out across the kitchen table.

He then calmly lit the lighter and threw it at his friend, turning him into a human fireball.

Chapter 26

JAMIE RYAN'S FATHER wept bitterly as he finished the first reading at his son's funeral mass. In life, he hadn't been able to forgive his son, but now, in death, he wasn't sure he would ever forgive himself for deserting him. But no matter what Jamie had done, no matter what anybody did, nobody deserved to die like that. It was all so brutal.

His wife stared straight through him as he regained his composure and returned to their pew. Her beloved Jamie was gone, so cruelly taken away from her. And now, here was her husband— her weak, spineless, gutless man—shedding crocodile tears. Where had he been for Jamie? For her? Well, now was not the time, but he would pay dearly for this. She felt nothing but hatred for him. As far as she was concerned, the marriage was over.

It was a very large funeral, though most of the people there hadn't come to pay their respects to the deceased. Jamie Ryan had been vilified in the press since Mary Kate died, and while there was some sympathy for the heinous manner of Jamie's death, the general view was that he got what he deserved. However, the Ryan family was a respected family, and the whole community had turned out to sympathise with them and show that they weren't going to turn their backs on them now.

Tim Bradley stood at the back of the church. He still wasn't sure whether he had done the right thing in coming to Jamie's funeral. He felt as if all eyes were staring at him. The whole church knew it was his son who had committed such a despicable act. It took all his courage to stay standing and not to run. The last few days had been so emotional. He genuinely thought he was having a heart attack the night the guards called and told him what Shane had done. Shane couldn't hurt anybody, let alone do what they were telling him. It was entirely inconceivable. The family doctor had to be called, but it turned out it was only an angina attack.

He felt so responsible. Why had he told Shane what Mary Kate said before she passed away? He should have known how devastated he was about her death. He should have insisted he come home with him from the courthouse. What sort of a father was he? He was physically and emotionally drained.

But he knew that it was time for him to step up to the mark. His son needed him now more than ever, and he was going to take control.

He was a man of considerable wealth and would do everything in his power to protect his son. He had already hired the best criminal lawyer in the country, Wesley Kelly, to defend Shane, and Wesley Kelly had already given the family some hope. In his opinion, it wasn't an open-and-shut case—there were a number of avenues to explore. They would indeed be putting up a very robust case.

Tim had no idea how he would be received by Dan and Mary Ryan. His son had taken the life of their son. He had made up his mind a day earlier to attend Jamie's funeral when he met all the Ryan family at Mary Kate's funeral. The sins of the son shouldn't be visited on the family. He knew this only too well himself.

A hush descended on the crowd when Tim approached the Ryan family to extend his sympathies.

"I'm sorry for your loss," he blurted out as he offered his hand to Dan Ryan. Tim knew immediately that his words sounded so empty, the kind of words you would say at some ninety-year-olds funeral, not at the funeral of a young man murdered by your own son.

Dan Ryan looked straight into Tim's eyes and said nothing. After a few moments' hesitation, he took Tim's hand in his two hands.

"I know you are, Tim," Dan replied kindly. "Thank you so much for coming. We really appreciate it, don't we, Mary?" he said as he looked at his wife.

"Yes, Tim, we do. Believe me, we—no sorry—I know how hard it is for you," she said as she turned and stared through her husband. "At least you have guts and know to do the right thing," she continued bitterly.

Tim nodded at Mary and went to walk away when she suddenly reached out and grabbed him.

"Tim, have you got to talk to him yet? Did he say anything? Why did he do it, Tim? Why?" She started to cry.

"I've no idea, Mary. I'm so sorry." Tim was now also crying. "They won't even let us see him yet," he continued, talking more to himself than to Mary. "They have moved him to Dundrum Mental Institution."

Chapter 27

THE JURY DIDN'T buy it. Wesley Kelly was indeed very impressive and persuasive. He was quite the orator and knew all the plays and angles. But they didn't buy it. The fact that Shane Bradley had committed the crime was not in dispute—the crux of the case was whether he was responsible for his own actions—the insanity plea.

Whilst it was true that Shane had been detained in Dundrum Mental Institution, it was done so at the request of Wesley Kelly, and the courts had given consent. The defence psychiatrists had fully evaluated him and were of the opinion that Shane had suffered a complete nervous breakdown. He was unresponsive and, according to their learned opinion, was in a psychotic state—he had lost contact with reality when he murdered Jamie Ryan.

Wesley Kelly had also relied heavily on the heinous cruelty involved in the crime and had argued forcefully that no sane person could kill another human being, let alone their best friend, in such a manner. It all sounded plausible until the prosecution had their turn.

The prosecution psychiatrists were very much of the view that, while it was very debatable whether he had lapsed into a temporary psychotic state after the crime, Shane Bradley was fully *compos mentis* when he callously took the life of Jamie Ryan. This was far from the picture the defence was presenting—an impulse crime that Shane committed upon hearing of the death of his cousin Mary Kate. The Prosecution produced numerous witnesses, including Jamie's solicitor Tom Dylan. They even subpoenaed Shane's father to prove that, while he certainly had been angry and very upset, his behaviour was not in any way irrational. The fact that the crime was committed some nine hours after he had heard the news further weakened Shane's case.

However, the killer blow was the evidence of the garage owner who had sold the petrol to Shane that night. He recalled that Shane had appeared in good spirits and had actually been quite chatty and good-humoured. This was not the crime of a madman. It was what it was—a premeditated, cold-blooded slaughter.

Shane Bradley was found guilty of the murder of Jamie Ryan and was sentenced to life imprisonment.

Shane had now been incarcerated for over forty years and was sitting opposite his solicitor Tom Dylan. Dundrum Mental Institution had been good for Shane and, over a period of time and a large quantity of drugs, the psychiatric staff had rebuilt him mentally. He was then transferred to the normal prison system. He now resided in the Midlands Prison, a Category C, low-level-security prison which housed petty criminals and a few old timers that were no longer considered a security risk.

Shane Bradley had done his fair share of hard time, but he was always treated well by the other convicts. Although he had little in common with most of them, being well-educated and from a wealthy background, his crime was considered a crime of honour among the criminal fraternity. He had avenged the death of his cousin and, therefore, didn't suffer the fate that would normally befall a prisoner so clearly from the other side of the tracks.

Also, the extremely violent nature of his crime and the fact that he stood at six-foot-four, weighing over nineteen stone, and had been transferred from the mental institution all helped with his standing in prison.

Although Wesley Kelly was an excellent lawyer, Shane never liked him. Against his father's wishes, he had dispensed of his services and set about retaining Tom Dylan. At first, Tom had refused point blank to have anything to do with him. He wasn't even sure if it was ethical to act for Shane, though that wasn't his primary concern. He was absolutely sickened to the core of his being by what Shane had done. Even to this day, Tom still struggled occasionally to deal with the heinous nature of his crime. But Shane knew how soft Tom was and laid it on thick and heavy until Tom agreed.

"Sorry, Tom. You said he wrote those anonymous notes around the time of Jamie's trial."

"Yes. That is what has been communicated to me. Professor Hamilton has said that he can prove that Jamie Ryan was an innocent man, who had nothing to do with Mary Kate's murder."

"Christ, Tom." Shane sighed as he placed both hands to his temples. "This is unbelievable. We need to meet him right away, right now, Tom," he said as he stood up. "We'll meet him wherever he wants. I'll organise a temporary day release from the warden if he doesn't want to come here. But why is he only coming forward now? After all these years? Can you set it up that we meet him today, Tom?"

"I'm afraid that won't be possible, Shane. He passed away last week."

Chapter 28

"YOU MUST REMEMBER this, Mr. Bradley, Jamie Ryan's death deeply troubled my late husband. It tormented him for the rest of his life. In a way, he felt responsible because he knew he could have prevented it. However, as I repeatedly informed him, he could not have known of your barbaric intentions."

The word 'barbaric' was delivered with venom. It stung Shane, as Mrs. Hamilton had intended it to do. Shane, Tom, and Mrs. Hamilton were now sitting in the parlour of her home, drinking tea from her best china cups. Even though she utterly despised Shane Bradley, there was absolutely no way Mrs. Hamilton would let herself down. She had been brought up to be better than that. But now, sitting opposite her was the man who had ruined her husband's life and, because of that, her life too.

Godfrey had been a serious man, but he was kind and attentive to his wife's needs and had loved her dearly. Jamie's plight had troubled him deeply. For the first time in the life of Godfrey Hamilton, he did not know what to do. On the one hand, he believed he possessed information that would prove Jamie Ryan was an innocent man. On the other hand, he was sworn to secrecy. He thought he had found the perfect answer by sending those anonymous notes, hoping to force Jamie's hand. But it hadn't worked. He was on the brink of doing what he believed was the right thing when Shane's actions made it all completely irrelevant.

After Jamie's death, Godfrey struggled to cope with his secret and had slowly turned towards alcohol as his crutch. He was not your typical drunk. In fact, quite the opposite. He was never abusive or disrespectful. The alcohol made him sullen, his guilt overpowering him. It was a gradual process that seemed to creep up on him but, before they realised it, Godfrey Hamilton preferred the company of his whiskey to that of his wife.

"Rome burned while Nero fiddled, Mr. Bradley," Mrs. Hamilton proclaimed.

"I beg your pardon, Mrs. Hamilton," Shane replied, looking to Tom for inspiration. Tom shrugged his shoulders quickly, hoping Mrs. Hamilton wouldn't catch him.

"The guilt of his inaction destroyed my husband, Mr. Bradley. I just want to make you fully aware that you took more than one life when you murdered that young man." She stared at him. She had been worried whether she would be capable of controlling her emotions when she finally came face to face with him, and now, found she was indeed struggling, the anger and bitterness growing inside her. Face to face with this monster. No, she would not, under any circumstances, allow herself to surrender to her emotions. She was made of sterner stuff.

"Anyway, that is not why we are here. I made contact with your solicitor in order to fulfil the wishes of my late husband. His instructions were very specific. Only when I am satisfied am I to release the information I have in my possession."

Shane's heart missed a beat. He was about to discover the truth. Mrs. Hamilton noticed the expression on his face and permitted herself a wry smile. If only he knew the magnitude of his task. Revenge is a dish best served cold.

She continued, "As Mr. Dylan has more than likely informed you, my late husband wrote to him during the trial telling him that

Jamie Ryan was innocent."

"With all due respect, Mrs. Hamilton, the letters were anonymous and lacking in actual information," Tom interjected. He couldn't let it go, the way she was telling it implied that he was inept and hadn't acted on vital information that had been brought to his attention.

"My husband had his reasons for that. As I was saying before I was so rudely interrupted..." She shot one of her infamous glances at Tom. "Where was I? Sorry, yes, my husband wrote those notes in the hope that they would spur Jamie into action, but alas, Mr. Bradley here decided he would play God." She paused for effect, this time staring Shane down until he duly looked away.

"Do you remember the film they made about you, Mr. Bradley?" Her question caught him completely by surprise. Where was she going with this?

"Yes, madam, I do, but I want you to know that—"

"It really doesn't interest me in the slightest what you want, Mr. Bradley. As I said, I am here to carry out the instructions of my late husband." Again the look.

"That film ultimately confirmed to my husband what he knew all along, the two aspects of the case that so deeply troubled him. Tell me, Mr. Bradley, how did the film end?"

He paused and looked to Tom for help, but it wasn't forthcoming. She waited for him to answer.

"It ended with Jamie's death," he finally whispered.

"Oh, let's not downplay it, Mr. Bradley. It ended with you slitting the throat of your best friend and then burning him alive. Let's call it as it is, Mr. Bradley, shall we?" She was actually starting to enjoy herself.

"Tell me, Mr. Bradley, does it bother you that, because of your actions, Mary Kate's killer got away scot free?"

"I beg your pardon?"

"My husband couldn't come to terms with that. Nobody ever went looking for the real killer. Everything stopped when you murdered Jamie Ryan. Nobody has ever attempted to find the real killer."

"I'm afraid I don't follow you." This time, Tom spoke.

"I think you do. Once Jamie died, Mary Kate's case died with him. It was all so convenient—after all, there was a confession. But you must remember, gentlemen, my husband knew as a certainty, that Jamie Ryan couldn't have done it."

"That's it. That's the phrase again. I remember now what was so unique about the notes," Tom enthused. "You didn't say that Jamie didn't do it, you said that Jamie couldn't have done it—two very different things." Tom also felt he was about to get closure on a great part of his life too.

Again, she ignored his interjection.

"My husband was going to come forward after you killed Jamie and prove that Jamie was innocent. But it dawned on him there would always be the sceptics who wouldn't believe. Furthermore, he was very mindful of the publicity that would follow and how it would portray him. As I said, he had his reasons, very valid ones, for not coming forward earlier. But he knew the papers would gloss over them and show him in a bad light. But above all, he felt in some way culpable for your crime. He dithered, and it cost Jamie his life. That's the way he saw it. Rome burned while Nero fiddled, Mr. Bradley."

She was very disappointed in herself as a tear rolled down her cheek.

"Jamie was dead, and eventually, Godfrey decided that he must take his secret to the grave. But it just kept eating away at him. Not only had you taken Jamie's life, but you also took away the most important thing that, in Godfrey's eyes, a man possesses. You took away his good name. Jamie Ryan died a murderer and a rapist, Mr. Bradley."

"Was he worried he would be prosecuted for withholding information, Mrs. Hamilton?" Tom tentatively asked.

"Absolutely not, Mr. Dylan," the strength returning to her

voice. "Godfrey had very good reason for not going public before Jamie's murder."

"But after the murder?" Tom asked.

"No good would become of it, Godfrey reasoned. Jamie was dead and nothing he could do would alter that fact."

"But why did he change his mind?" Shane blurted out. He was doing his best to stay quiet and let her tell them what she knew. But it was taking so long.

"I suppose you look at things differently when you're about to meet your Maker," she replied coyly. "Gentlemen," she proclaimed, "my husband's last will and testament is very specific. I am to release the information in my possession that proves Jamie Ryan's innocence. But first, you must fulfil one condition that permits me to release the information."

Neither man could breathe let alone speak.

"Shall I continue?" Both men nodded in unison.

"As my husband saw it, Mr. Bradley, you created the problem, so you solve it. Furthermore, gentlemen, time is not on your side as my health is ailing too." She stood up to get the door.

"I don't understand what you want from us?" Shane said.

"It's quite simple, Mr. Bradley. Godfrey insisted that you find the real killer of Mary Kate."

Chapter 29

"I'VE SPOKEN TO the powers that be, and it is as we thought it would be. Even if we did manage to get the information that Mrs. Hamilton claims she possesses, the authorities have no desire whatsoever to re-open a case that's well over forty years old. Apart from that, they also said they just wouldn't have the resources to devote to it," Tom informed Shane.

Two weeks had passed since their meeting with Mrs. Hamilton and, as agreed, Tom had contacted and made representations to anybody who would give him a hearing in order to get Mary Kate's case re-opened.

"Are there any legal avenues open to us to force Mrs. Hamilton's hand?" Shane asked, more out of hope than anything else.

"There are a few possibilities, but I fear that if we attempt to coerce her in any way, she will just clam up and, like her husband, take her secret to the grave. We've really nothing to threaten her with. Just suppose we somehow managed to get a court order, and, by the way, I think our chances are very slim, do you honestly think she'll comply? She has nothing to fear—a frail old woman near the end of her days. What are they going to do to her and does she even care? Anyway, it doesn't answer the real question."

"What do you mean, Tom? Of course, it does," Shane asked puzzled.

"It may or may not prove Jamie's innocence, but it doesn't get us any closer to Mary Kate's killer."

"So it leaves us exactly where we thought we'd be," Shane said.

"Yes. The official line is that her case is closed, and they are not looking for anybody in relation to it. The case closed upon the death of their prime suspect. As it stands, we don't have access to the resources required to re-open the case ourselves, unless you make the phone call," Tom concluded.

"And sell my soul?"

"If that's what it takes."

"Okay. So be it."

Later that night, Shane made the phone call that he knew was inevitable the day he left Mrs. Hamilton's parlour.

Chapter 30

NED BRANNIGAN ARRIVED at the restaurant forty-five minutes early and set about finding a quiet secluded table where they wouldn't be disturbed. The location for the meeting wasn't ideal. He had hoped she would have agreed to meet him in private, but she had insisted on a public place, and he made no real attempt to persuade her otherwise. After all, it had taken over three weeks to get her to agree to meet him. He took his seat, making sure it faced out towards the door so that he could see everything, and then he did what he did best. He waited.

Ned had received his briefing from Bill Owens or the Big O as he liked to be called, about six weeks ago and had now been in Ireland for over five weeks. Big O was a short, stout man, but he liked his nickname as he thought it showed that he was just a regular guy, just one of the boys, a team player. Nothing could be further from the truth. He was an egotistic bully who was very used to getting his own way. As head of one of the largest studios in LA, he used his power ruthlessly and crushed anybody who stood in his way. You didn't cross Big O.

This was Ned's largest assignment to date from the Big O, but also, the most difficult. He had contemplated turning it down, but he knew that it would be both futile and disastrous even to raise the possibility. Big O was his biggest client. He paid handsomely, but you did not refuse him. But to solve a murder case that was over forty years old, with no new evidence and no new leads? A very big ask. If he did manage to solve the case, he could literally write his own cheque, but what would be the consequences of failure? Big O didn't tolerate failure and, no matter what he said, it would be the end of Ned Brannigan P.I. He had seen it all before. Anyway, it was all academic. He just couldn't refuse the assignment.

Ned was also delighted that the case would take him to Ireland and for at least six months. After all, he was half Irish and had always planned to spend some time in the Emerald Isle before he died. The fact his half-Irishness was three generations ago on his Grandfather's side didn't diminish his Irishness in his eyes. He was and always had been a proud Irish American.

Ned couldn't recall exactly the first time he had 'worked' for the Big O, but it was certainly a long time ago. He had been a rookie in the LAPD. Ned learnt the ropes and knew when to turn a blind eye. He became the Big O's favourite cop one night when he was called to a situation involving a high-class hooker and one of Big O's leading men. Things had gone wrong. The hooker had ended up with a broken nose and was going ballistic. She wanted charges pressed, but Ned was finally able to persuade her to accept a financial compensation instead. She relented only when Ned showed her the cocaine he claimed he had found in her bag. She would, of course, be charged and immigration would have to be informed. He told Big O it would cost twenty grand to pay her off. Everybody was happy. Big O was delighted the problem was solved, the hooker was happy with her fifteen thousand dollars, and Ned was happy to skim off five grand for himself, to add to the three-thousand cash Big O had given him.

Their arrangement worked very well for both of them. If a 'favour' was required or something needed fixing, Ned Brannigan was the man. Ned's career had also flourished in the LAPD. By the time of his retirement fifteen months ago, he had reached the rank of Police Captain, which had allowed him to facilitate the movie industry. Everybody was happy.

"I'll do it because I know how much this means to you, Big O," Ned had said to him. "But I ain't guaranteeing any results. It was a very long time ago, and I don't have the contacts over there. But because it's you, man," Ned finished and embraced Big O. He knew how to play him and to appeal to his already inflated ego. Ned supposed you didn't get to be in Big O's position without having a big ego.

"Thanks, Ned. I know you won't let me down." There it was—the veiled threat. "We solve this, and it's going to be massive, man. Shane Bradley has already promised me. I even have a signed contract from him, whatever exclusives I want," Big O continued. "You thought my first film was good? Wait till you see what we can do with Bradley's full cooperation. Wow, can you imagine if the Ryan fella didn't do it? What a film that would make!"

"Don't get your hopes up, Big O," Ned said, but he knew it would fall on deaf ears.

"One last thing," Big O said, not even attempting to acknowledge Ned's comment. "Whatever it takes, Ned, you know what I mean? Whatever it takes."

Ned did indeed know exactly what he meant.

Chapter 31

"THANK YOU, MRS. O'DONNELL, for agreeing to meet me," Ned said as he stood up and offered his hand. She looked at his hand but made no attempt to shake it, forcing Ned to withdraw it. He had guessed that she would be prickly. *At least, she turned up,* he said to himself.

"Would you like to order some lunch?" he asked her when she was fully seated.

"No, thank you. I'm not hungry. Actually, I'm really uncomfortable with this. I think I've made a terrible mistake coming here. I should leave," she blurted out and went to get up from the table.

Time for action. No more Mister Nice Guy.

"SIT DOWN NOW," he commanded. "You go now, and you won't see a cent of the money." Ned waited. With all his years of experience interviewing and interrogating people, he knew how to read people, when to push and when to back off. Now was definitely a time to push.

"We have a deal." Ned now lowered his voice to show his caring side, an old trick. "I promise you, Mrs. O'Donnell, this won't take long. I only have a few simple questions for you, and then you can go, and I swear I'll never bother you again."

It hadn't taken Ned long to prepare his strategy to tackle his current assignment. Being in a foreign country without his usual network of connections had proven only a minor inconvenience.

However, Ned correctly reasoned that people were the same the world over. He did his homework and sourced the 'Ned Brannigan' in Dublin. Between them, tracking her down was simple. Preparing the 'file' on her had taken a little longer than it would have in the States, but Ned wasn't going to rush anything. The file was quite comprehensive, and Ned wouldn't start without it. To him, it was essential, and the level of detail proved an invaluable tool. It invariably pinpointed stress points, and the information gleaned would be used to determine the best way to proceed. Everybody had secrets.

One of Ned's favourite weapons of choice was appealing to a person's greed. It generally delivered quicker results than the power of fear. He quickly established, after acquiring Mrs. O'Donnell's bank statements and financial records going back five years, that the pressure point was the old reliable—money. The bank had recently bounced a cheque, and the next instalment of her youngest daughter's college fees was due within the next month. Her debts didn't seem too serious to Ned, but debt is a relevant term. A little money would go a long way with Mrs. O'Donnell.

"Here's your money," he said as he slid the envelope over to her. "Ten thousand euro as agreed. You can count it if you like." Ned would ordinarily have bargained harder with her, but time was of the essence. Anyway, the expense claim to Big O would read fifteen thousand euros, and Big O wouldn't even bat an eyelid, as long as Ned ended up getting the right result. In Ned's eyes, Mrs. O'Donnell was critical to the case. He had to get the truth from her.

"Thank you," she replied sheepishly.

"Hey, you're doing nothing wrong here." He smiled reassuringly, but her eyes told him it was futile.

"It's just that it took me so long to get over it, and now you're going to drag it all up again. I'm not sure if I'm strong enough to deal with it."

"You are. Trust me," he said, smiling again. He really didn't care if she was or not. He needed the information she possessed, and it was of no concern to him how it affected her. What did she think he was? Her priest?

"I've dealt with many victims of sexual assault, and believe me, you're stronger than you think you are," Ned continued.

"You think that's what it's all about, don't you?" she said with contempt. "Nothing could be further from the truth."

She now had his undivided attention.

"Do you mind?" he asked as he took out his recorder and notebook and placed them on the table.

"Eh, I didn't know you would be recording our conversation. I'm not very happy about it," she replied.

He ignored her response and commenced his questioning.

"Let's start from the beginning. How did you know Jamie Ryan?"

She looked at the recorder and back at him. He pretended not to notice. She hesitated, but then answered, "We went out together for a short while."

"Went out together? I'm sorry I'm not one hundred percent sure what that means. It's not an expression commonly used in the States. Do you mind clarifying?"

"We were boyfriend and girlfriend," she obligingly clarified.

"Okay. For how long?"

"It was a very long time ago. I'm not exactly sure, a few months. Two, three months, maybe."

"Can you be more specific?" Ned knew the devil was in the detail.

"Very well. For over fourteen weeks to be precise," she replied forcefully. Ned looked up and recognised the look that came across her face. There was very little that slipped by Ned Brannigan when he was questioning somebody. Ned now knew this relationship had meant a great deal to her.

"Why did it end?" He now stopped taking notes and watched her carefully.

"It just did. Look, it was a very long time ago. We were kids really. It just fizzled out, the way these things do at that age," she replied, but he immediately spotted the tell of a lie.

His next move was critical.

He reached out and snapped the envelope out of her hands and stood up.

"All right, forget about it, lady. I'm not here to have my time wasted," he said as he started packing up.

"I don't understand. I'm not wasting your time. I'm trying my best, and I'm answering all your questions and—"

"You're lying to me and, what's worse, you're a bad liar," he cut across her. "Either we have a deal or not, your choice. But one more lie, and I'm out of here. *Capice?*"

He stared her down until she answered slowly, "Okay."

"Okay then." Ned sat down again. He went to give her the envelope again but, as he placed it in her hand, he tugged at it and reminded her, "The truth from here on in, and no more dicking me around. Agreed?"

"Agreed. I'm sorry," she responded.

He now had her exactly where he wanted her. From now on, she would be like putty in his hands.

"Why did the relationship end?" he calmly continued as if nothing had happened.

However, before she answered, she edged her chair slightly back from the table and placed the envelope in her handbag that she now had firmly clasped in her lap. He noticed it. It was his job to notice everything. Good move, he thought.

"To be totally honest with you, I really don't know. We seemed to be getting on so well and, then suddenly, out of the blue, he ended it."

She waited for him to ask his next question, but he sat there tight-lipped, waiting for her to continue. As she had feared, all the guilt associated with that part of her life, and the subsequent murder of Jamie Ryan, came flooding back. In an instant, she was overwhelmed by it all. Her counsellor had repeatedly told her that it was good to cry, that she should go with her emotions and not try to suppress them—which is exactly what she did. Tears flowed freely down both cheeks.

Ned had anticipated tears at some stage, but not from such a benign question. He immediately took out his handkerchief from his lapel pocket and handed it to her.

"There. Take it. It's clean," he said. She thanked him and dabbed her eyes. Ned noticed that the couple three tables away were now looking at her with concern. That was the problem with a public place. It wasn't a controlled environment. It was open to external influences. He decided he would have to tread softly and slowly from now on. Otherwise, some Good Samaritan might stick their nose in and ruin it.

"He ended it out of the blue? No big row? No signal at all that everything wasn't right between you?" he probed.

"Yes." She was struggling to regain her composure. "I'm sorry for getting upset." She gently sobbed. "I'm not crying for some old childhood romance." She tried to laugh. "But, at the time, I genuinely thought I loved him and then, everything that happened after that..." She trailed off.

Her words blindsided Ned. He was expecting a bitter woman, or maybe a victim who had learned to come to terms with her past, but not this. Here she was confessing her love for Jamie Ryan. Ned was confused but remained totally calm. She wasn't making total sense, but he'd let her continue. He would mop up any loose ends before she left.

"I often think what might have been, you know? But we can't dwell on the past. We must live in the here and now." The tears had now stopped, and the strength was returning to her voice. Ned had no doubt this lady had received extensive counselling, and it was the counsellor now speaking through her. Mrs. O'Donnell was right—this was certainly still very painful for her.

"When did Jamie Ryan end the relationship?" He needed her to focus and move on.

"Exact date? I'm really sorry, but I'm not sure. It was so—"

"No, no. Sorry. Obviously not the exact date, but when, roughly, relative to the night in question?" He should have been more specific, he scolded himself.

"The night in question! That's a good way of putting it. I presume you mean the night that Mary Kate was attacked?"

"Yes."

"Jamie ended the relationship exactly two weeks before Damien's twenty-first birthday party, which was the night Mary Kate was attacked" she coldly replied.

"Okay. Thank you. Can you remember why Jamie said he was ending the relationship?"

"The reason? What's that got to do with anything? I don't see how that can be relevant."

Ned was about to point out that it wasn't up to her to decide what was relevant or not but opted to stay quiet. He gave her a look which she knew meant, 'just answer the questions you're asked and let's get this over with.'

"The reason," she sighed, "the reason he gave, well, I can't remember his exact words, but it was along the lines of the old cliché, *it's not you, it's me.* He said he had to deal with some issues, and he couldn't handle a relationship until he got them resolved."

"I see. Did he elaborate or tell you what the issues were?"

"No. I pushed him hard on it. I thought at the time that he was just trying to be nice, and it was a load of bullshit, and I wanted the real reason. I told him he at least owed me that. You have to remember, Mr. Brannigan, I never saw it coming. One minute, we're having a great time and the next, we're back in his parents' kitchen, and he's dumping me. I was mad about him. I genuinely thought I was in love with him, and you know how intense young love can be."

Ned nodded, not because he agreed with her, but because he knew it was the appropriate response, and he felt it might ingratiate himself more with her.

"So, he wouldn't tell you. Did you push him on it?"

"Yes. Oh, yes. I told him that I could help him with whatever was bothering him, that we were a team, a very good team together and, whatever it was, we'd be able to handle it."

"And?"

"And nothing. He just wouldn't go there. For a split second, he went very quiet, and I could see that he was seriously considering telling me what was on his mind. But then, he just shook his head. He had made his decision and that was that. We were finished as a couple. Jamie was always a very determined young man when he wanted to be. I even suggested that we take a break rather than finish completely, but he was having none of it. He just said he'd call once he got his head together. That was the expression he used," she concluded.

"Mmm, I see. Could you take a guess at what was bothering him?" Ned asked.

"Now?" she replied.

Ned was annoyed with himself at his amateurish question and sought to structure the question that he wanted to have answered.

"Not now, but back then. Back then, what did you think his issues were that made him feel he had to end the relationship?

"No idea then and no idea now, to be honest. The only thing that crossed my mind at the time was that he was drinking a lot. But then again, we all were. We were all so young and carefree. We had left school and were really enjoying our freedom."

"Could he have been involved with another woman?" Ned asked. His question seemed to register something with her.

"I don't think so. I did wonder. I always wondered actually, whether he was in love with Mary Kate. They were really so close.

But she was such a sweetheart. She would never do that to another girl. I remember—and this was before Jamie, and I broke up—having a drunken conversation with Shane and telling him how jealous I was of Mary Kate and how well herself and Jamie got on. But he laughed and assured me they were more like brother and sister than anything else."

"Shane?" Ned quizzed. He already guessed she was talking about Shane Bradley, but he wanted to draw her out more.

She gave him a puzzled look. Was that a question or a statement?

"Shane Bradley, I presume. How well did you know Shane Bradley?"

"How well did I know Shane?" she repeated the question to herself. "Very well. He and Jamie were as thick as thieves. They were practically inseparable, so I saw a lot of Shane around that time. I was convinced Shane would know what was bothering Jamie, and he'd be able to talk sense to him. But he was totally shocked when I told him that Jamie had ended it with me and what he had said. He swore that he didn't know what was going on, but he said that he would talk to him. I could tell he was concerned, but also very puzzled. My God, Shane genuinely was the last person you would ever think would hurt anybody. He was such a gentle giant. What he did was truly shocking, and I feel so guilty—"

Ned moved swiftly to cut her off. He couldn't allow her to go down the path of self-pity.

"Do you think that Jamie raped and murdered Mary Kate?" His question stung her back to the present.

She looked at him, actually stared through him. She had known that he would ask her that question, and yet it seemed to shock her. She realised that, even after all these years, she still had no answer. She suddenly felt very exposed and vulnerable. She felt like bolting.

"Could I have a glass of water please?" She was desperately trying to buy time.

160

"Mrs. O'Donnell, we are coming to the crux of it now. A few more minutes, and we'll be finished. Just think of the good that will come from the money." Ned tried to get her to stay focused.

"And what good will the money be to me if I can't cope again, Mr. Brannigan? I worked so hard and for so long to put it all behind me, and now, you come in here with your Yankee accent and dredge it all up again. No amount of money is worth this," she shouted at him and slammed her fists against the table. The restaurant fell quiet.

Shit.

Shit.

The last thing he needed right now was a hysterical woman in the middle of a popular restaurant at lunchtime. He wanted to reach over and slap her hard in the face, but even he knew that wasn't an option. An apology might work, or it could push her over the cliff.

"I'm sorry," he said as he reached in and cupped his hands around hers. "I'm so sorry. I really didn't mean to upset you. I wasn't expecting this reaction." He levelled with her, throwing caution to the wind. "I'm very confused. My understanding was that Jamie Ryan had also attacked you, and you were lucky to escape with your life."

"It wasn't like that. It was never like that," she screamed at him as she pulled her hands away and jumped up from her seat. Her chair went flying as she bolted from the restaurant.

"No. Not like that," she shouted back at him as she reached the door.

"Then why did you tell them that he did?" he shouted at her. All eyes were now staring at him, but he was oblivious. What had just happened?

"They made me do it," she bawled, running into the street.

Ned Brannigan calmly picked up her chair and returned it to its upright position before grabbing her handbag that she had dropped on the floor.

Chapter 32

"I DON'T CARE if she's the Queen of England. Just find out what she knows. It's gloves-off time. I told you before, whatever it takes."

Owens and Brannigan were sitting across the coffee table in Brannigan's suite in the Shelbourne Hotel, discussing Mrs. Hamilton and whether she had a bearing on solving the case. Brannigan had initially thought she was bluffing when she informed Shane Bradley that her health was ailing, but now he had obtained a copy of her medical records. Not good. Not good at all. Only a matter of weeks, six months at best. She had no children, another avenue closed off. Sometimes that could be good leverage with a reluctant parent.

"And another thing, explain to me about the O'Donnell broad again, would you? I still can't believe you just let her walk out on you like that. And you've let nearly a week go by without contacting her. What the fuck is that about? I gave you this assignment because I thought you were the best in the business. Was I wrong?" Big O continued.

"No, you're not wrong. It's best to let her come back to me. And she will, believe me."

"Why should I believe you? You haven't really set the world alight with your performance to date, have you? I swear to God, Brannigan if you fuck this up ..." Big O shook his fist at him but didn't finish his sentence. He didn't have to.

The fact that this was the first time Big O called him by his surname was not wasted on Brannigan. Bill Owens was having a rant, not just any rant either, but the mother of all rants. Ned Brannigan had seen it before but never as bad as this. It was also his first time on the receiving end. Ned felt the anger rise up inside him, and he was so tempted to tell this fat, arrogant bastard where to go, but he knew he had to suck it up and take it. There was no other way.

Owens wasn't even particularly angry with Brannigan. He was absolutely livid with Shane Bradley, but even Bill Owens knew he couldn't bully him. Owens had arrived in Ireland unannounced the day before and had played Shane Bradley for a fool. Big mistake.

He had gone to visit Bradley in prison earlier that day. As far as Owens was concerned, it was game on, and all systems go. Shane was amused to see him, and even more amused when he told him why he was there.

"My people are very close, very, very close, to solving this whole mystery, Shane, my man, and when they do, we need to be able to hit the ground running, if you know what I mean." He then gave him one of his legendary Big O knowing winks. He was well able to manipulate people, and Shane Bradley would be no exception. Big O thought he could charm the Devil himself if it came to it. "So, what we need to do is get some interviews recorded so that when we crack this case—and believe me, Shane, we're very close—all we'll need is the final interview, and we'll be ready to go."

Big O drew breath and continued. "We'll record three hour-long interviews, just background stuff mainly, and then we'll edit it down as we see fit." No reaction—that's a good sign, thought Owens. "And, don't worry Shane, a deal's a deal, and I'm a man of my word so there'll be no questions about Jamie's mur..., sorry, Jamie's last night. We'll record that once the case is solved, and we're very close, Shane, my man," he finished. Holding both his hands up, he squeezed his thumbs and index fingers so that they were nearly touching. "That close, man." Big O couldn't help the smug look on his face. He was so convincing. No wonder nobody turned him down.

"Really," Shane said in an impressed tone. "That close?" He imitated Big O's gesture.

"Yep. That's what I hear." He had him now. Time to move on. "Now, I was thinking we should probably get the background interviews, the soft interviews, done sooner rather than later, maybe over the next few days?"

"That sounds like a plan," Shane replied.

"Great. Well, I'll just call—"

"But I prefer the original plan," Shane interrupted. "How about you solve the case like you said you would? And I'll then be at your complete disposal. Let me spell it out for you. I have no intention of talking or meeting with you again until you can prove to me who murdered Mary Kate. I hope I am making myself perfectly clear."

Big O was about to speak, but Shane continued.

"And one last thing, Mr. Owens. I don't appreciate you insulting my intelligence like this. No more stunts. Just solve the case if it can be solved. Otherwise, get out of my life."

Shane then walked out of the room leaving Big O speechless for once in his life.

Chapter 33

NED BRANNIGAN WOULD usually not even have contemplated doing a job like this himself. On his home turf, it would be subcontracted out to people he knew and trusted. The job would be done right, and more importantly, it couldn't be traced back to him if anything went wrong. But this was different. There was nobody in this city he could trust. The last thing he needed was some crackhead fucking everything up. It wasn't just a simple burglary. The house would have to be searched from top to bottom, and he wasn't exactly sure what he was looking for.

It didn't take much surveillance to establish Mrs. Hamilton's pattern, and he settled on her Monday night bridge game as his best opportunity. She left the house at 7.20 p.m. and usually returned around 10.45 p.m. He reckoned that gave him plenty of time.

Mrs. Hamilton didn't disappoint him and left the house right on time. He gave it ten minutes to allow for any mishaps or forgotten umbrellas before he disabled the alarm and entered through the back window. With all his police experience, Ned was quite the expert at searching a house from top to bottom, and he immediately went to the master bedroom where he reckoned there may be a hidden safe. He was right. The safe was badly concealed behind some clothes at the back of one of her wardrobes. It was a cheap combination steel safe, mounted on the wall. Easy pickings, thought Brannigan as he laid out his tools. He bet with himself that he could crack the safe within ten minutes.

The adrenaline was now pumping through his veins in anticipation. Brannigan was enjoying himself and was about to find out what she knew. However, he was still very sceptical whether this would help solve the case. It might somehow prove that Jamie Ryan was innocent, but would it lead him to the killer? He doubted it. He was going to find out very shortly, he told himself.

He allowed himself a wry smile when the safe door flew open after nine minutes. It always amazed him, the stupidity of people investing in cheap, standard safes. They were like an open invite to a professional thief—although, he surmised, they probably did the job if some junkies were robbing your place.

The moment of truth had arrived. His heart skipped a beat as he emptied the contents of the safe onto the bed. There, along with some jewellery was a standard A4 brown envelope.

"Hello, is there anybody there?" Mrs. Hamilton called out from the hallway.

Jesus.

On her way to the bridge club, she had received a text from her bridge partner saying she was feeling poorly and would have to cry off. Unfortunately, her phone was in her handbag, and she only got to read the message at the bridge club. Undeterred, she waited to see if there was anybody whom she could partner, but there was no one available. She decided to return home and was now standing in her hall, feeling very vulnerable. There had been a spate of burglaries in the neighbourhood of late. When she had gone to turn off her alarm, she was shocked to realise that it was already off. Mrs. Hamilton never doubted herself and knew, with absolute certainty, she had set her alarm. Her blood froze when she saw that the door from the kitchen to the hall was open. That was never the case.

Without hesitation, she pressed the panic button attached to her wrist.

"Help me, please. I have an intruder in my house," she told the voice from the monitoring station.

"I'll inform the guards right now. I suggest, if you can, you leave the house immediately for your own safety," the voice said.

"I will do no such thing. This is my home," Mrs. Hamilton replied. What a ridiculous request, she thought. "They had better leave. I'm going nowhere."

A loud siren screeched through the house.

Brannigan knew he had to act fast. He cursed himself for being too engrossed in his work. He should have noticed her returning, but the drilling had drowned out all sounds. Anyway, no time for that now. There was only one option. He pulled the balaclava over his head and made a run for it. But not before he grabbed the envelope.

She met him on the stairs. Before she had time to react, he charged at her, knocking her flying. She was no match for him. He knew time was of the essence and didn't even look back to see how she was. Stupid old cow, he thought. However, just as he reached the open front door, he spotted a concerned neighbour walking up the driveway. This time, the contest was more even, but Brannigan had the element of surprise and caught the man with a left hook that put him down. Brannigan realised the punch came at a price. He had broken something in his hand.

Not for the first time that evening, Brannigan cursed himself, this time for his lack of planning. He had become too complacent and hadn't even bothered planning an escape route. He definitely couldn't return to his car, nor could he keep running with his face covered by a balaclava. He could hear the police sirens in the distance.

Brannigan got lucky. He came to a laneway and ran into it, checked behind him to make sure nobody was following him, then slowed down to a walk. He removed his balaclava and threw it into the nearest garden, making no attempt to try to hide it. He didn't have time. Within minutes, he was on a crowded Luas tram heading back to Dublin city centre.

Shit, that was close, he told himself. He would have to be a lot more careful in future. And he'd have to get some ice for his hand as he felt it throbbing in his pocket.

But at least he had the envelope.

Chapter 34

BRANNIGAN BEGAN TO ponder the possible consequences of his actions as he walked the short walk from the Luas terminal at St. Stephen's Green to his hotel. He wasn't particularly concerned about the man he had floored with his trusty left hook—he looked reasonably fit and healthy, and Ned had heard him groan as he hit the ground. But it was a totally different matter when he considered Mrs. Hamilton. She was a frail old woman with a serious medical condition, and she had taken a very heavy fall. He shuddered when he recalled how she had literally bounced off him. The heat would definitely come on if she were seriously hurt or, at worst, killed.

Ned Brannigan typically remained calm, but he was now very much out of his comfort zone. What if somebody had seen him in the laneway? They would easily find the balaclava and match his DNA if they found him. Time to get out of town until he could establish how she was. No time like the present, he told himself, as he walked briskly across the lobby of the Shelbourne hotel, his injured hand firmly in his pocket. He'd collect his belongings and check out tonight. Better safe than sorry.

"Mr. Brannigan," a male voice called after him. Brannigan quickly assessed his options and decided that making a run for it was futile. It was too crowded, and he wouldn't get very far. He calmed himself down before turning around.

"Mr. Brannigan," the man called again.

"Yes," Brannigan replied, now facing the man.

"My name is Peter O'Donnell. I believe you've met my wife," he said as he gestured towards the lady standing to his right, Siobhan O'Donnell.

The timing couldn't have been worse. Ned knew that she would be in touch sooner rather than later, but he had expected a phone call, not an ambush in his hotel lobby. And he hadn't factored in the husband. He tried to get a read from the husband, but he couldn't get the measure of him just yet. Was he here to make sure she got the money this time round or was he here to remonstrate with him over the treatment of his wife? Either way, he didn't have time for this right now.

"Follow me," Ned commanded, turning on his heels and heading for the lift. They duly obliged—Ned concluded the husband was there for the money.

Brannigan sat opposite them in his suite and deliberately waited for them to speak. After all, they had sought him out.

After a few moments hesitation, Peter started. "My wife has told me all about your meeting, and I'd just like to say—"

Brannigan cut him off immediately. He didn't have time for this and had now fully assessed the type of man Peter O' Donnell was. He certainly wasn't a threat. Any man who says, 'I'd just like to say...' is as good as asking for permission to speak, and at this point in time, Brannigan refused permission to the wimp.

"Either you guys want the money or not? Your decision. I'm not here to be fucked about again." He glanced briefly at her. "You want the money? It's still on offer, but the deal's the deal. You want to walk? Walk."

"Now look here, Mister." Peter stood up. "We didn't come here to be spoken to in that tone or manner. We—"

"Sit back down now before I put you sitting down," Brannigan

172

hissed at him. "What did you come here for?"

He directed the question at her, but Peter replied, "You really upset my wife last time. You brought up things that she had worked so hard to deal with, to put behind her, stuff that has haunted her for more than half her life. It's been a very difficult time for her."

"I'm sorry if I upset you," Brannigan said to Siobhan before walking over and opening the door.

"Now, if you'll excuse me, I have another pressing engagement that I must attend." He held the door open for them and waited.

"No," Mrs. O'Donnell finally spoke. "I'm not leaving without my money. I've earned it, and you owe it to me," she shouted at him.

At last, he thought. "Will you finish the interview?" Then, dropping his voice, "I assure you, we'll be no more than ten to fifteen minutes, and then I'll never bother you again." He prided himself on knowing when to close a sale, closing the door after she nodded her head. As least, he could close off this part of the investigation. His earlier panic about Mrs. Hamilton was easing. He would still be leaving this evening but reasoned another fifteen minutes wouldn't matter. Besides, she is probably okay, he reassured himself.

"First things first, Mrs. O'Donnell. Here's your handbag you left behind and..." he retrieved the envelope from her bag "...here's your cash as earlier agreed. You can count it if you wish."

This time, the O'Donnell's left nothing to chance. Peter O'Donnell placed the envelope in his inside jacket pocket.

"Thank you," whispered Mrs. O'Donnell.

"Right then. I only have two questions, and then we're finished. All right?" Brannigan said as he glanced at his watch. Fifteen minutes max, he told himself.

"Fine," she replied, and he could see that she was steeling

herself. He hoped there would be no repeat of their last meeting. He reasoned she had had plenty of time to prepare herself.

"Okay then. First question. At our last meeting, you said that it wasn't like that. You made an allegation of attempted rape against Jamie Ryan shortly before the trial, and now you're saying that it wasn't like that. Please explain fully." He deliberately went with an open-ended question as he felt it appropriate at this juncture, but he had one eye on his watch. If she started waffling or straying from the point, he would hit her with rapid and more direct questions.

She took a deep breath and squeezed her husband's hand.

"There was a particular incident that occurred between my wife and Jamie Ryan ..." Peter began, but Ned interrupted.

"Not from you, sir. I'm sorry, but I need to hear it directly from her," Ned said calmly before continuing. "Look, Mrs. O'Donnell, I'm sure you fully anticipated that I was going to ask you that, and you've had plenty of time to think about your answer. Just take a deep breath and tell me all about it. Then we can all move on." Ned waited.

"Yes, you're right." Another deep breath, and then Ned finally got his answer.

"When I was going out with Jamie, there was one particular night. We both had a lot to drink and landed back at my parents' house. They had gone to Kerry for the weekend, and my younger brother was staying at a friend's house, so we had the house to ourselves. Anyway, how do I put it? We were engaged in heavy petting, and things were moving quite quickly. We were both young and, before long, neither of us had many clothes on." She glanced at her husband, who nodded at her to continue. Ned stayed silent.

"Then, after a little while, Jamie seemed to tense up and became quite agitated. He was now kissing me very forcefully, not passionately as before, and he was getting rough, somewhat physical, in a way he had never done before. I got scared and pulled away from his embrace. But then I was shocked when I saw

174

his face. It was contorted in anger. He really frightened me, and I jumped up and ran to the door. I told him he was really scaring me and that I wanted him to leave immediately."

"What did he say?" Ned asked.

"He said nothing at first. He just looked at me. Then he said he was very sorry if he scared me. He didn't mean to, and if I wanted him to leave, he'd go. He was very genuine, and there wasn't a trace of anger in his voice. He returned to the gentleman that he always was," she finished, breathing a sigh of relief.

"Is that it?" Ned asked incredulously.

"What do you mean?" her husband asked.

"If you interrupt one more time, or say another fucking word in this room, so help me God, I'll put you through the fucking window," Ned shouted, grabbing him by his shirt. Ned genuinely didn't have time for this shit. He then pulled Peter's face close to his. "Do I make myself clear? Don't even say yes, just nod." Ned could tell that he was frantically thinking what he should do, but Ned knew exactly what he would do.

Peter O'Donnell duly nodded.

Ned pushed him back into his seat.

"Again, Mrs. O'Donnell, is that it? Was that your attempted rape?" Ned couldn't believe how angry he was actually getting himself.

"Yes," she answered. She was trying to stay strong, but her voice quivered.

"So, let me get this straight. You're two young kids having a good time, and he's getting a bit excited, pushing maybe for a bit more action. You slap his hand, so to speak, and he says sorry and stops. And that's your attempted rape?"

"Yes but—"

"Did he have an erection?"

"I beg your pardon."

"Did he have an erection? Mrs. O'Donnell, we're all adults here."

175

"Of course, he did."

"So it's probably fair to say that it was a bit more than heavy petting. Might foreplay be a better word to describe what was going on?"

"You could say that."

"And you didn't break up with him after that. You told me he broke up with you, one night out of the blue."

"Correct."

"So you mustn't have thought too much of it if you stayed being his girlfriend."

"At the time—"

"Mrs. O'Donnell, now I fully understand. You know in your heart and soul that Jamie Ryan never attempted to rape you. Anything that ever happened sexually between the two of you was entirely consensual. Am I right?"

She nodded.

Ned looked at his watch. Six minutes gone. Good, doing all right on time.

"Thank you. Last question. How did it come about that you signed a statement saying that Jamie had attempted to rape you when you knew he hadn't?" He had anticipated she would recoil from the question, but there was now a steely resolve in her. She just wanted to get this over and done with.

"Okay. When Mary Kate was raped, and Jamie confessed to it, I began thinking about that night and perhaps I was a lucky girl. Maybe he had considered raping me that night. When I was interviewed by the guards, I made the stupid mistake of mentioning it to them."

"You were interviewed?"

"We all were. Anyone who was at Damien's twenty-first birthday party that night. They interviewed us all."

"Of course." Brannigan was very familiar with what happened at the party. Much had been made of Jamie's threat that night and of his violent behaviour. It would have been standard police work to get statements from everybody who attended.

"Anyway, the guards were very interested in the fact that I used to be Jamie's girlfriend and kept pushing me for any other information that I could think of. Initially, I wasn't going to mention it—like you said, I hadn't really thought too much of it at the time. But they kept pressing me whether there was anything else they should know, and I decided to tell them about that particular incident, for what it was worth."

"And?"

"And that was that. Then, a few days later, I got a call from the young guards who interviewed me saying that the officers in charge of the case wanted to speak with me, and they were calling around to collect me. I told them exactly what I'd told the other guards, but they were different. They were very aggressive and kept trying to put words in my mouth."

"I see." Brannigan could very easily picture the scene. He had been there on many occasions himself.

"At first, I refused to sign their statement. I told them they were twisting my words. But then, out of the blue, the older guy chilled me to the bone. He said that he hoped to spare me this, but Jamie had already told him all about that night, and I had indeed had a lucky escape. He then went into detail as to what Jamie had said he was going to do to me that night, graphic detail. I nearly got physically sick. He told me that Jamie was a very sick pervert, and it could easily have been me lying on the hospital bed."

"Did you believe him?"

"What do you think? Of course, I believed him. You have to remember I was only a child at the time, and these were two senior police officers. It never even occurred to me they could be lying. Jamie had also signed a confession."

"Sorry, please continue."

"Well, that's pretty much it. I did ask them why they needed my statement when they already had a signed confession. They said it would ensure that Jamie wouldn't retract his confession. At that stage, all I wanted was out. I couldn't sign it fast enough. They had really frightened me."

She exhaled slowly, and as far as she was concerned, she was now finished.

She stood up to leave.

"Mmm…" Ned took in everything she said. "Do you believe them now? Do you think Jamie said all that to them?" Ned finally asked.

"Does it matter?"

"A very good question. I suppose it doesn't," Ned replied as he stood up and looked at his watch.

Twelve minutes. Time to go.

There was a loud knock on the door.

"Open up. Police."

Mrs. Hamilton's envelope. If they found him with it, he was a goner. He had to act fast.

Chapter 35

"MY, MY, QUITE a little gathering we have here," the young guard said, surveying the scene. Brannigan's heart was beating so fast he was fully sure they could see it pounding under his shirt. Why hadn't he left when he had the chance? How did he get himself into this mess? This was bad, real bad.

"The suspect is here, Commissioner," the young guard called out and then stood to attention at the door. The Commissioner? Brannigan was now totally confused. Even if Mrs. Hamilton was dead, surely the highest ranking guard in Ireland would not be investigating it himself. Something wasn't quite right. But then Brannigan remembered when Commissioner Cullen entered his hotel suite.

"Ms. Williams. What an unexpected surprise," Cullen addressed Mrs. O'Donnell. "It's been such a long time," he said, offering his hand.

"Indeed it has," she replied nervously, accepting the handshake.

"And I presume this is your husband," Cullen continued. The two men shook hands.

"Now, while I would love to stay and chat, I have very grave matters to discuss here with Mr. Brannigan," he told them as he gestured towards the door.

The O'Donnells didn't need to be asked twice and quickly went to gather their belongings. Brannigan seized the opportunity and buried Mrs. Hamilton's incriminating envelope in Mrs. O'Donnell's handbag before helping them leave. It was a weight off his mind when he saw them walk straight past the young guard who was now posted as sentry outside his room. But he wasn't out of the woods just yet.

Brannigan was struggling to rationalise the situation that he now found himself in alone in his hotel suite with the Commissioner. However, he knew a shakedown when he saw it and quickly began to calm down. If there was something seriously wrong with the old dear, the Commissioner would not be here, and he would be in cuffs by now.

"Would you care for a drink?" Brannigan asked, confidence oozing out of him.

"No, thank you." Cullen laughed. "I'm afraid this isn't a social call. It's not a one-cop-to-another chat."

Very clever, Brannigan thought. A nice way of letting him know that Cullen had done his homework and was fully aware who Brannigan was. Brannigan deemed him a worthy opponent. Let the games begin.

"You enjoying your stay in Ireland? It's been a few weeks now," Cullen asked.

"Yes. It's quite a beautiful country you have here," Brannigan danced back.

"Well, I think now you've overstayed your welcome, and it's time you went back home. Don't you agree, Ned? I presume you don't mind me calling you Ned."

"Not in the slightest. That's the name my parents gave me," Brannigan replied, digesting Cullen's order.

"Well, then, Ned," Cullen leant into him, "you came, you saw, and I presume you now realise that there's nothing here to keep you from going home. As I said," Cullen's big red face was now inches from his own, "it's time you left this little island of ours."

"It that a request or an order?" It was so unusual for Brannigan to be on the receiving end, he was actually enjoying it. He certainly wasn't in the least bit intimidated.

"Ned, please listen to me, for your own good. I don't like repeating myself. Now, we've been more than fair and accommodating to you. We've left you alone since you arrived, let you dig and probe, and upset very vulnerable people. But now the fun is over, and you're pissing me off. So, as I said to you, it's time for you to leave."

"I know exactly who you are, and you don't scare me. You're one of the—"

"Ned, don't insult me. I would be very disappointed if you didn't know who I was. For what it's worth, not that you give a damn, we got the right man. Now, I'm asking you nicely, from one cop to another, to leave it be."

Brannigan was relishing this. Here was the head of the police force in Ireland pleading with him to drop his investigations. He had overestimated him. He wasn't a worthy opponent after all.

"I'm afraid I can't oblige," he replied. "I have unfinished business here. I think I'll stick around for a while. In fact," Brannigan now leant into him, "I think I'll probably extend my vacation."

"Very well." Cullen sighed and backed off. "You want to play it like that? I wonder will you come down to the station and assist us with our enquiries into an incident that occurred earlier this evening."

An incident! Brannigan now knew that Mrs. Hamilton was all right. If she had been killed or seriously hurt, Cullen would never have dared to come himself—it would have been too risky to interfere with the investigation. Brannigan was now emboldened by this realisation.

"Fuck off, Cullen. You have absolutely nothing on me. If you did—"

The force of the punch knocked him to the ground. But, as he attempted to stand up, Cullen stood on his injured left hand.

"God, that hand looks a bit swollen. Maybe you should put ice on it." He sniggered as Brannigan squealed in pain.

"Now you listen to me good, Yank. I don't give a shit about some breaking and entering and maybe an aggravated assault thrown in. But…" Cullen bent down and pulled Brannigan's head up by the ear, "what really concerns me are your connections with the dissident republican group, the Real IRA."

"The what?"

"You heard me. The Real IRA. You mightn't be familiar with our anti-terrorist laws over here, but the Real IRA is a proscribed organisation. Membership normally carries a prison sentence of anywhere between ten to fourteen years. And, because of the Troubles, there is no requirement for a jury. Just a judge and the word of a high ranking guard are deemed sufficient evidence. As I said, we have had you under surveillance since you arrived. I briefed one of our top guys in the Anti-Terrorist Unit, actually a very good friend of mine, and they're ready to lift you. I told them I'd give the order within the next forty-eight hours."

Cullen now moved all his weight onto Brannigan's injured hand.

"Forty-eight hours, you fucking Goddamn Yank," he roared in his ear. "Do we have an understanding?"

Brannigan nodded. Cullen was indeed a worthy opponent, in fact, a superior opponent, and one who had all the cards. He knew when he was beaten.

Chapter 36

"TO THE AIRPORT," Brannigan said to the taxi driver.

He hadn't slept well the night before. He hated losing, and this defeat would cost him dearly. It was certainly early retirement for him—Big O was not a forgiving man. Initially, when he awoke, he thought about the events of the previous night and calmly tried to rationalise his options. Perhaps Commissioner Cullen was bluffing and was merely trying to scare him off. Get out of Dodge, indeed! Who the hell did he think he was? Ned Brannigan didn't scare easily. However, he got a very uneasy feeling after googling Irish anti-terrorist legislation. Everything that Cullen had told him was true. But would he actually go to such lengths just to stop him digging into a case that was over forty years old? Brannigan didn't think so, but could he afford to take the risk? The consequences of calling it wrong were dire.

Brannigan decided to call his contact in Ireland to see what he could find out about the Commissioner. Before he had time to speak, the contact told him, in no uncertain terms, that he wouldn't be able to help him in any way going forward. He was on his own. "Furthermore," he threatened Brannigan, "you make sure that my name doesn't come into this. You've crossed the wrong people over here. I understand you were given a warning last night. Trust me—it is very much in your interests to heed that warning. Once they go down a certain path, it's next to impossible to stop it. Too many people then become involved." The phone then went dead, and Brannigan realised he had better book a flight fairly quickly. He didn't really know his contact that well, and he definitely didn't trust him. He correctly assumed his contact was right now informing Commissioner Cullen of their phone call. It also occurred to him that his contact was expecting his call and was instructed to reinforce the message. Again, he wasn't wrong.

After he had booked his flight, Brannigan decided to take a stroll around St. Stephen's Green. It wasn't that he needed the fresh air or wanted to experience the bustle of Dublin one last time. He had an ulterior motive. It didn't take him long to spot them and, to be honest, they weren't trying to be in any way inconspicuous. They were overtly following him. That also made up his mind for him whether he would attempt to retrieve Mrs. Hamilton's secret from the O'Donnells. He would have to pull strings from afar and hope she wouldn't discover it herself in the meantime. He would have to act fast, but the top priority at the moment was to leave the country.

"Do you mind if we take the Port Tunnel rather than head out through Drumcondra? There's a big game in Croke Park today and the traffic there will be a nightmare," the taxi driver asked.

"What's the catch?" Brannigan knew from experience there had to be a catch if a taxi driver was asking.

"There's a toll involved. It will cost you an additional six euro but will probably save you at least forty minutes."

"Well, let's splash out, shall we?" Brannigan grinned.

Brannigan was deep in thought, contemplating the best approach to adopt with Big O. He was resigned to the fact that their relationship would be at an end. But what he now needed to do was max out, to try to take Big O for as much as he could. He wouldn't be able to string him along for too long. Big O was not a stupid man, and Ned desperately needed to come up with a plausible reason for why he had left Ireland in such a hurry.

He would have to incorporate it into the case somehow.

"There are some interesting sites along this route," the taxi man interrupted his thoughts. He must have picked up on his American accent, Brannigan thought. Well, at least he's trying to earn his tip. But just when Brannigan was about to tell him he didn't want to be disturbed, and could he just get him to the airport, the taxi driver said something that now had Brannigan hanging on to his every word.

"You ever see that film *Shane and Jamie?* I'm sure that's the name of it."

Brannigan sat upright in his seat. Was this a setup?

"Yes," he answered cautiously.

"Well, a lot of it was set around here. But you see that side street there?" He pointed to his left. "The actual apartment where the girl, Mary something or other, was murdered is just down there. It's in a small block of—"

"Pull over," Brannigan shouted. Was this fate?

"Eh. You sure? What time's your flight?"

"Yes, I'm sure. Now pull over," Brannigan commanded.

But as they pulled over to the kerb, Brannigan noticed the car three vehicles back also pulling in.

The scene of the crime. Why hadn't he thought of it before? But then, what could he possibly learn from visiting a crime scene some forty years after the crime? Absolutely nothing, he reasoned. But then again, what had he to lose? You never know when you get your lucky breaks. Anyway, Cullen had given him forty-eight hours, so he was well ahead of schedule. It was worth a try.

"You know the apartment?" Brannigan asked.

"Yes, I do. As a matter of fact, the apartment block itself is quite a tourist attraction."

Less than one minute later, Brannigan walked defiantly from the taxi and pressed the intercom on the apartment. However, his defiance was very much weakened when he observed one of the men in the car trailing him talking into his handset. The car had pulled up blatantly behind the waiting taxi. One of the men got out and stared at him while the other continued talking on the radio.

"I see," replied Commissioner Cullen as the guard updated him. Cullen had already been briefed that Brannigan had packed up and was in a taxi, heading for the airport, he presumed. He was delighted with the news, though he knew that Brannigan wouldn't scare easily and was geared up to act if required. He breathed a sigh of relief but had also issued instructions that he was to be personally updated immediately if there were any unscheduled stops.

"Give me that address again, please?" Cullen asked. The address meant nothing to the guard, who wasn't privy as to why Brannigan was a threat, but Cullen was fully aware of its significance.

"Thank you. Please keep me informed," Cullen then terminated the conversation.

Stupid man, he said to himself as he banged his desk in anger. *Well, if that's the way he wants it, that's the way he'll get it.* Cullen decided he wouldn't waste any more time. Forget about forty-eight hours. He called in the favour owed to him by the Head of the Anti-Terrorist Unit.

"It will take a bit of time to get the paperwork right, but we'll pull him as soon as we can. Do you want this to go the whole way or do you just want to scare him? "

"The whole way," Cullen replied.

Brannigan hadn't even considered what he was going to say in order to gain access to the apartment. He had decided it would be more prudent to leave now when the male voice that came over the intercom shocked him.

"Come in. I've been expecting you. Why did it take you so long?"

Chapter 37

BRANNIGAN WALKED THE few short steps to the apartment in utter disbelief. He had been expecting him? But who was he?

He was none the wiser when the young man opened the apartment door and beckoned him in. Brannigan studied him hard. He was absolutely positive he had never met him before. He was young, no more than twenty-three, Brannigan reckoned, about five-feet-ten-inches and of medium build, and very much the student type, judging by his clothes and the ponytail. Brannigan racked his brains, but literally, he had no idea who he was or what connection he had to the case.

"Sorry I snapped there. It's just that I've been waiting all day for you, and I thought you would have been here last week. I do have things to do, you know. Anyway, I'm Greg. Would you like a cup of tea or coffee?"

Brannigan was utterly baffled. He had arrived here totally by chance and yet Greg was expecting him.

He actually thought he would have been here last week!

Greg. Greg. Greg.

No matter how many times he said the name to himself, it simply meant nothing to him.

Who was he?

What did he know?

A thought crossed his mind. Was this man working for Cullen? Maybe the cops outside were in touch with Greg? Perhaps Greg's instructions were to stall him until Cullen decided his next move.

However, it didn't fit. Brannigan couldn't read him and decided to trust his gut instinct. The kid was genuine. This was Mary Kate's old apartment and, in all likelihood, Greg's connection was to Mary Kate.

But, much as he wanted to, he decided not to rush things. He would draw the kid out.

"Coffee, please. I'm sorry I'm so late."

"That's not an Irish accent. Where are you from? America? Or Canada? I'm sorry I can't really tell them apart."

Strange. Surely, if he knew he was coming, he would have known his name and a lot of detail about him. Maybe not, Brannigan concluded. He might just have known that there was a private investigator employed by the studio who would visit.

"American."

"What brings an American over here? How do you take your coffee? Milk? Sugar?"

Very strange. Whatever game Greg was playing, Brannigan decided to play along for the moment. But he was getting very uneasy. It very much felt like he was stalling him. But the kid seemed so sincere. If he was putting on a performance, he deserved an Oscar.

"Black and no sugar please." He pretended he didn't hear the first question.

Greg let it go.

"Coffee coming right up. Now where do you want to start?"

"I'll just have a quick look around, and then if you could answer a few questions? Maybe we might solve this mystery once and for all."

"Alleluia to that. It's been driving me crazy. But, and I don't mean to be rude, where are your tools? Do you want to get them out of the van while I make the coffee?"

His tools!! He didn't imagine that Brannigan would be looking for forensic evidence after such a time lapse, did he? Maybe the kid meant a notebook or possibly a recording device? Brannigan wasn't sure.

"Nah, I don't need any tools. I've a great memory, and I'll write it up later. This really won't take very long. Actually, I'm on my way to the airport. I've a taxi waiting outside," Brannigan said.

"What? What's going on?" Greg's demeanour instantly changed. He was becoming agitated, and Brannigan scolded himself for giving away too much information.

"Now look here. I'm a patient man, but there are limits," Greg began, but he was interrupted by a call on his mobile phone.

"Ah, your office," he said as he looked at the caller ID. He stepped back away from Brannigan to take the call.

Maybe this was the signal from Cullen. Had he misread him? Was Greg stalling him all along? Was he part of the set-up?

But none of it made sense. Brannigan was only here by chance, an impulse decision at the last minute. Unless the taxi driver was in on it also? Should he make a run for it?

"What do you mean tomorrow? Your guy is standing right in front of me. Christ, you guys are so inefficient. You don't even know where your people are."

Brannigan strained to hear the other side of Greg's phone conversation but couldn't. However, he noticed a big change in Greg's body language. He was listening intently but also staring at him. He seemed scared and had taken another step back, away from Brannigan.

"You sure?" Greg asked. "Okay, I see. I'll call you back," he said as he terminated the phone call.

Greg stared straight at him, and Brannigan noticed that he had clenched his fists.

"Are you here to fix the plumbing?" Greg finally asked.

The penny finally dropped. The whole complex web of connections he had imagined fell away, and all Brannigan could do was laugh. But Greg still hadn't figured it out, and his demeanour hadn't changed.

"I'm sorry. No, I'm not here to fix the plumbing," Ned eventually replied when he regained his composure.

"Well then, who are you and what are you doing in my apartment?" Greg demanded.

"Remember you buzzed me in. Look, Greg, I'm sorry for laughing, but I hadn't a clue what you were on about, asking me about my tools and telling me how late I was. I'm an American," he hesitated before continuing, "…a tourist and—"

"A tourist! I was expecting the plumber, and I just buzzed you in. You must have thought I was mad," Greg said and started laughing too. "Man, wait till I tell the boys down at the pub, they'll get a great laugh out of it." He started mimicking himself. "And where are your tools?"

Both men now saw the funny side of the simple misunderstanding and enjoyed the moment.

"Do you get many tourists?" Brannigan finally asked.

"A good few. In general, they're just outside taking photos of the building, but you get the odd one or two asking can they come in and look around."

"Do you normally let them in?"

"Not really anymore. I've been here a good few years, and you just get sick of it. At the start, I used to let them in, but they're mainly nutjobs with way out conspiracy theories who feel compelled to bore me with them. You seem normal enough, though."

"Thank you. I'll take that as a compliment. Do you mind if I have a quick look around?"

Brannigan knew Greg was now fishing, but he wasn't prepared to be truthful with him.

"I know it's a terrible imposition on you, but I'll be very quick. Like I said, I have a taxi waiting outside."

Greg noticed that Brannigan wasn't prepared to tell him why he was there, but he wasn't particularly bothered.

"Work away. I better get back to those plumbers. Their man got delayed on his last job. That's their excuse anyway, and he can't make it until tomorrow morning. They think I've nothing better to do than sit around waiting for them all day. I'm tied up tomorrow. I better ring my Mum and see if she can let them in."

"It's a pain all right. Do you have much trouble with the plumbing?"

"Yes. It seems to be never ending. As far as I'm concerned, it was never right from day one."

Interesting.

"Greg, listen, I'll be out of your hair in no time. But would you know where Jamie Ryan and Mary Kate were when the cops arrived that morning?"

"I was told that Jamie Ryan was there—" He pointed to a spot in the sitting room. "And Mary Kate was just over there." He pointed to another spot not far away. "I really don't know any other details, other than what everybody else knows. One of life's greatest mysteries, I suppose," Greg concluded as he walked away to call his mother.

Brannigan looked around the room. Something wasn't quite right. He struggled to recall the contents of the detailed files that he had received from Tom Dylan's office.

He was so close he could smell it. But it just wouldn't come to him.

He looked over at the window. What was wrong with the scene?

"Mam can't do it." Greg disturbed him. "I'm just going to pop over to Peter to see if he's around tomorrow morning. I hate to rush you, but are you nearly finished?"

EUREKA!

191

Brannigan knew he was now in for the biggest payday of his life.

"I love you, man!" he exclaimed as he hugged a very bewildered Greg. "You've been so helpful. I'm on my way."

But Brannigan's euphoria was very short lived.

The SWAT team was getting into position.

Chapter 38

"WHAT THE FUCK just happened there?"

"I beg your pardon, Mr. Brannigan. What do you mean?"

"You know what I mean. This is bullshit—that's exactly what I mean."

"But, Mr. Brannigan, I thought you'd be pleased. The judge granted you bail."

"Yes, but those terms! God damn it."

Brannigan was furious. He had spent the last three weeks on remand in Portlaoise prison. Apart from reneging on giving him forty-eight hours to leave the country, Cullen was true to his word, and Brannigan had been very publicly arrested that afternoon in Mary Kate's old apartment.

"But where are all the checks and balances?" Brannigan continued his rant at his lawyer. "I mean, on his word alone, without any other corroborating evidence whatsoever, you've taken away my liberty, and now I face a trial where I could be locked up for over ten years. It's totally preposterous."

"The 'he' you refer to is the Head of our Anti-Terrorist Unit. Anyway, consider yourself lucky that you're not over in your own country. At least, over here, you're entitled to a trial. Okay, it's not in front of a jury, but there's a judge, and you have the right to plead your case. I can safely say your treatment here, and our checks and balances compare very favourably to Guantanamo Bay, do you not think? And you're just after getting bail!"

"Sorry, I don't mean to sound ungrateful. It's just that I didn't think I'd have to surrender my passport and to sign on daily and—"

"Would you prefer to be back in Portlaoise? I'm sure that wasn't particularly pleasant for you, especially since the media broadcast that you are an ex-cop. I'll be in touch once we get a trial date. Good day to you."

Cullen really fought dirty. The deliberate leaking of that information was designed to make his period of incarceration as uncomfortable as possible. He had achieved his objective. Brannigan had had to be very careful in prison. He was despised by the criminal fraternity and treated with deep distrust by the few remaining dissident republicans who knew he wasn't one of them.

However, his time in prison had given him plenty of time to think. Cullen would fight tooth and nail to make sure that Mary Kate's case would never see the light of day again. He had made absolutely no attempt to contact Brannigan since their chat in his hotel suite. He was warned, and he hadn't heeded the warning. Simple as that. And now Brannigan had to face the consequences. Brannigan had to expose the truth and bring Cullen down in order to hopefully gain his freedom.

Brannigan hadn't risked doing any work on the case in prison. Whether he was becoming paranoid or not, he assumed they were watching his every move and monitoring his phone calls. He needed access to the internet and to his files, especially the file that Tom Dylan had given him. But he wasn't prepared to disclose his hand, and so he had to wait it out. He had now lost three weeks.

Big O wouldn't be happy with the delay, but he would be very interested in this latest twist. He had tried to contact Brannigan in prison, but Brannigan told him it wasn't safe to talk. He would explain everything when he could. But Brannigan had also decided that he couldn't tell everything he knew to Big O, not yet anyway. Big O had loyalty only to himself, and if Brannigan was no longer of any use to him, he would cast him aside like an old ragdoll. In actual fact, he suspected that it might suit Big O better if he was sent down. He could see it now—Big O pontificating on Oprah about how he had finally solved the case as his special investigator rotted in an Irish prison on a trumped-up charge. He might even give him an exclusive from prison!

Brannigan went to the nearest phone store he could find and bought himself one of those Prepaid Ready to Go mobile phones. He then went down to the river Liffey and promptly threw his iPhone in.

Now we're back on track, he thought. Time to catch the killer.

He called Tom Dylan to arrange a meeting with Shane Bradley.

Chapter 39

"I AM AS certain as I've ever been of anything in my life that Jamie Ryan did not kill Mary Kate," Brannigan announced and then paused for effect. He was in the Visitors Room in the Midlands prison and could feel Tom Dylan's and Shane Bradley's eyes staring at him. They were listening intently but, given Shane's previous meeting with his boss Big O, they were both extremely suspicious of him. Like all of Ireland, they were fully aware of Brannigan's latest difficulties.

"I also firmly believe, based on my own recent experiences …" Brannigan allowed himself a wry smile "…that the guards also know this. That's why Commissioner Cullen, who was one of the leading guards on the case, is prepared to stop at nothing to halt my investigation." He sat back and waited.

Tom finally spoke.

"Mr. Brannigan—"

"Please, call me Ned."

"Very well, then, Ned. I have two questions. Actually three. Can you prove that Jamie didn't do it? And is that the same proof that Mrs. Hamilton possesses? And the most important question of all—do you know who killed her? Sorry, that leads to another question. Can you also prove who killed her?" Tom finally finished.

Brannigan pondered the questions as Shane and Tom held their breath. They both sincerely hoped that closure was imminent.

"I have a theory—"

"A theory! Here we go again. All you have is a theory, and you guys expect me to—"

"Please let me finish, Shane, and then you can ask any questions you want. As you know, this case is also very important to me because of the difficulty I'm now in. I think if I—we can solve it, they will then have no choice but to drop the charges against me. If you think, when I'm finished, that it's all bullshit, then I promise you I'll be on my way. Is that fair enough, Shane?"

"Yes. Sorry. Please continue."

"Firstly, thank you, Tom, for sending me over another copy of your files. As I suspected when I got out of prison the other day, all my files relating to the case have disappeared. I'm sure I can answer all your questions, Tom. I know who did it, but I will need your help to prove it."

"Are you serious?" Shane couldn't contain himself. "After all these years, you think you know who killed her. And you can prove it."

Shane had been entirely consumed by her murder for all these years. Was he finally going to find out the truth? However, he was overwhelmed by the occasion.

Tom gently placed his arm around his shoulder but said nothing to him. Nothing needed to be said.

"Okay, Ned. Please, let's hear your theory," Tom said.

"Actually, it's a bit more than a theory because it's based on facts—facts contained in your files."

"My files! But I know every inch of those files. I've been through them so many times. I'm certain I missed nothing." He looked over at Shane. "Shane, I'm so sorry…"

"Relax, Tom. Everybody missed it initially. And then, when

Jamie confessed, there wasn't any need to look any further. But I think that's why Cullen is trying to frame me with this ridiculous terrorist charge. He also figured it out, and I would say probably many years ago. But if the real truth comes out, it will be the end of his career. He might even end up going to prison himself."

"In my files?" Tom was still in a state of shock.

"Let me explain," Brannigan began as he spread out a series of photos on the desk.

"Do you recognise the photos?" he asked.

"Yes." Both men answered in unison.

"They're pictures of Mary Kate's apartment," Shane said.

"The crime scene so to speak," Tom added.

"Correct. Now, when the cops arrived, Mary Kate was still alive, so it wasn't a murder scene. Their top priority was to help her, to give whatever medical assistance they could until the ambulance crew arrived. So these pictures were taken later on, but you can clearly see the blood stains on the carpet. See there?" Ned asked as he pointed to one of the photos. Both men nodded.

"Okay. So we're in agreement that's where she was lying when the cops arrived?"

"Yes," Shane answered.

"And from Cullen's and Flood's statements …" Brannigan then produced copies of their statements. He had already highlighted the relevant sections. "Jamie was lying just here, right beside Mary Kate," he said as he pointed to the photo again.

"Okay."

"Okay, so please bear with me on this. We've agreed we've established the position of the two bodies, for want of a better word. Now, Shane, do you remember where Mary Kate's apartment was in relation to the main entrance to the apartment block?"

"Yes. I think so anyway. It was a very long time ago, but I'm fairly sure she lived on the ground floor. You went in the main entrance, and her apartment was the first one on your left."

"Thanks, Shane. That's correct. So if you come out of the apartment block, you'd turn right to walk by Mary Kate's apartment. First of all, you'd walk right by her kitchen window, and then by her sitting room window. You with me?"

"Yes."

"Okay. Now please look at the pictures again. What do you see?"

Both men followed Brannigan's lead and zoned in on the windows.

"Kitchen blind is halfway up," Tom said.

"Sitting room curtains are drawn," Shane chipped in.

"Exactly," Ned said smugly as he then handed them another copy of a document from the files.

"Here's a copy of the transcript of the 999 call. In those days, they didn't record them. The neighbour who made the call said he was walking by the apartment and thought he glimpsed a body through the kitchen window. He then looked through a gap in the curtains in the sitting room and saw her. But that just isn't physically possible. Through the kitchen window, you can actually see some of the sitting room, but only a small corner of it. And you definitely couldn't see the section where Mary Kate and Jamie were lying. To see them from the outside, you'd have had to see them through the sitting room window. And you can see that the curtains were firmly drawn. So if the neighbour couldn't have seen the bodies, how did he know they were there?"

"Oh, my God. So he must have done it. He must have killed her?" Shane jumped up and asked.

"Exactly," replied Brannigan evenly.

"Not so fast," Tom announced. Tom had come a long way from his first criminal case with Jamie and was now quite the seasoned pro.

"The only thing it proves—no, it doesn't even prove that—the only thing it *suggests* is that the neighbour didn't see them as he was walking by. It doesn't prove anything else. For example, he may have heard a struggle the night before and was too ashamed he hadn't called the guards then. Maybe he felt he could have helped her. Or maybe he saw a shadow, or a reflection, from the kitchen window. Or possibly the guards or somebody else closed the sitting room curtains for whatever reason. Maybe, with the curtains opened, the light was bouncing around the room, and they needed to close them to get a better quality photo. It proves absolutely nothing, and certainly not that he killed her. I'm surprised at you, Brannigan, you've been around long enough you ought to know better," Tom finished in disgust.

Shane returned to his seat, crestfallen.

Brannigan then took up again.

"You're right, Tom. I, like you, have been around the block a few times. But I've learnt one thing that has always stood to me. If it smells wrong, generally, it is wrong. And this stinks. But let's park the neighbour for a minute. There are two reasons why Jamie was the chief suspect in the case. The first was that he was found lying beside her body in a locked apartment, and the second was that nobody else, apart from Shane, had a key, and there were no visible signs of a break-in. Both of them were very valid reasons to treat him as a suspect, but they don't amount to a scintilla of evidence. It is all circumstantial, and the investigating guards would have known that. It would have been laughed out of court. However, the only real evidence they had was that Jamie had given them—his signed confession. And I firmly believe, along with anybody else who's given this case more than a cursory look, the confession was beaten out of him."

"Can you prove that?" Tom asked.

"No. You will never break the code of silence that surrounds such a confession. But I've studied the copies of the custody records, and they just don't stack up."

"What do you mean? They're flawed?" Shane now asked.

"No. The exact opposite. They're perfect, and that's the problem. They show absolutely everything happening when it was meant to happen—meal breaks, interview breaks, rest breaks, all of it. In reality, it never happens like that. There's always some complication, something that goes wrong. And guys, you have to remember we are dealing with a different era, the Good Old Days as us cops would call it. There was no CCTV, no tape recording of interviews, no ombudsman, no nothing. Just two old-fashioned tough cops against a young, scared kid—a kid who had never been in trouble with the law in his life. What amazed me is that it took them so long to break him."

"Jamie was very resilient, very bloody-minded when he wanted to be," Shane said of his old friend.

"That's all very well, Ned," said Tom, "but there's nothing new in the theory that the confession was beaten out of him. Your 999 call is interesting and leads to unanswered questions, but I'm afraid it doesn't get us any nearer the truth. The fundamental question in the case has always been about access to the apartment. Everybody has said there is no way Mary Kate would have let somebody in at that time of night. So, if anyone other than Jamie did it, how did he get into her apartment? That's the crux of the case."

"I couldn't agree more, Tom. Now, before I answer that, I'm going to tell you how we're going to solve this case." Brannigan paused to allow his words to sink in. "What you're going to do, Tom, is to go talk to the neighbour who made the 999 call and get him to confess." Brannigan moved back in his chair and waited for their response.

Shane was first to unload.

"For Fuck's sake, Brannigan. What a ruse. You had me going for a while. You can tell your boss to stick it. Stop playing me. You tell him, all bets are off. I don't want to hear from you again," Shane shouted as he thumped the table and stood up to leave.

Tom was equally annoyed.

"Pathetic," he said as he started to gather up his papers.

But Brannigan just sat there with a big stupid smile on his

face. He knew that one of them would eventually ask the question, and then he would have them.

It was Tom who duly obliged.

"And, purely as a matter of interest, I presume you know where I can find this man so I can just go out to him and get him to confess to a crime that he has got away with for over forty years?" Tom sneered as he slammed his briefcase shut.

Bingo.

"As a matter of fact, I do. He has gone under various different names, but you'll find him in Strangeways Prison in Manchester where he's serving life for the rape and murder of at least nine women."

That stopped both men in their tracks. They returned to their seats.

"Sweet Jesus," Shane finally uttered.

"Are you sure?" Tom eventually asked.

"One hundred percent positive. But we have a problem. Now we all know everything we have doesn't prove a thing. We have no evidence at all against him. That's why it's up to you, Tom. We need you to go and talk to him, get him to confess. It's our last chance to finally put this case to bed and clear Jamie's name once and for all. Without that confession, we have nothing," Brannigan concluded.

"Why me? Surely you would be much better at that sort of thing than I would be. That's what you've spent your whole life doing. I really think you would be a better man for the job than I would."

"I totally agree, Tom. But Cullen is all over me like a rash. Under the terms of my bail, I can't leave the country. I even had to surrender my passport."

Tom sat there weighing up the options.

"You'll do it, Tom. Please say you will. Jamie might have been innocent after all," Shane said as he buried his head in his hands.

"Of course, I will, Shane. Don't worry," Tom replied. "But Ned, one question."

Ned was expecting it.

"How did he get into her apartment?"

"I have a theory. I think......"

Chapter 40

"OKAY, TOM, WE'RE all set. Now remember, he's incredibly clever, and the game with him is all about winning. He will do everything he can to get one over you. Another thing to bear in mind, he has never expressed one ounce of remorse for the hideous crimes he committed. He's a cold-blooded psychopath, so don't think for a moment that you can appeal to his better nature. He doesn't have one," Chief Constable Terry Fairbrother concluded.

"Thanks, Terry. You've been so helpful. Wish me luck," Tom replied.

"Good luck. You're going to need it. I'll tell the wardens to bring him down now. Are you sure you don't want me to sit in on the interview?"

"I'm not sure at all, Terry, but I think initially, I'll talk to him myself and see how I can get on. Maybe if that doesn't go well, I'll get you to sit in on the next one."

"I wouldn't bet on him granting you another one, Tom. I had to work very hard on him to agree to meet you in the first place. As I said, it's all a big game to him. I really hope you get the answers you came for." Terry finished, shook Tom's hand, and then left Tom alone in the interview room in Strangeways.

Tom tried to calm himself down and to control his breathing. He was painfully aware how much depended on the next twenty minutes or so. He had to orchestrate a situation whereby this evil genius would actually tell him the truth about what had happened that night. If he failed, the questions would remain unanswered forever. Ever since Brannigan outlined his theory to them ten days ago, Dylan committed every waking minute preparing for this interview. He had read everything that was ever written about Peter Fletcher, his real name, although he had used one of his many aliases, Peter Winterbottom when he was in Dublin all those years ago.

Tom had travelled over to Manchester two days earlier to meet Chief Constable Terry Fairbrother, the man credited with finally ending Fletcher's reign of terror. Terry Fairbrother was a decent, old-fashioned cop who had worked his way up from the beat. He couldn't have been more helpful, but he wasn't convinced that Fletcher was their man.

"It could be him all right. But it really doesn't fit his M.O. All of his rapes and murders were extremely violent. He brutally beat all his victims and killed them at the scene of the crime. There wouldn't have been a question of them surviving an encounter with him. You say Mary Kate died afterwards in hospital. That's very unlike him. And the young man, Jamie Ryan, was also in the apartment and wasn't harmed in any way. Again, very unlike Fletcher. The Fletcher I know would have enjoyed killing them both. Actually, the only thing that makes me think it could have been him is the fact that he made the 999 call. As I said, he likes to play games."

The moment of truth arrived as Fletcher was escorted into the interview room.

Fletcher had recently turned sixty but could easily have passed for a man in his late forties. About five-foot-ten and of slender build, with white hair and piercing blue eyes, it was obvious to Tom that he took very good care of himself and liked to work out.

In actual fact, he looked quite the gentleman.

"Mr. Fletcher, my name is Tom Dylan. Thank you very much for agreeing to meet me at such short notice," Tom said as he stood up and offered his hand.

"You're most welcome. Besides, I couldn't refuse a request from my good old friend Terry, now could I? I was actually hoping he would be here today, give us a chance to catch up on old times," Fletcher said cheerily as he ignored Tom's hand and plonked himself down on the chair opposite Tom.

Tom sat down opposite him and took a deep breath.

"I'm here to ask you—"

Fletcher immediately cut across him.

"Terry told me why you're here. You're Irish, aren't you? Love the Irish. Good old sports, they are. You want me to help solve Mary Kate's case."

"Yes, please. You—"

Again, Fletcher jumped in.

"Mary Kate. Mmmmm, yes, I remember her well. Such a *sweet innocent* girl." Fletcher spoke very slowly, his eyes rolling back up into his head in dreamlike recall. Suddenly, his gaze snapped back to Tom, and he smiled. It had the desired effect, making the hair on the back of Tom's neck stand up.

"But I'm afraid, Tom, you're putting two and two together and coming up with twenty-two rather than four," Fletcher continued.

It was now Tom's turn to interject.

"You didn't see them from outside the apartment. You lied to the police."

"You calling me a liar?"

Tom hesitated for a brief second.

"Yes, I am," he declared, but he wasn't sure if Fletcher had taken the bait.

"That's not very nice of you, Tom, and you after coming the whole way over for me to help you. And then you insult me like that! Tut, tut." Fletcher sneered at him.

"Did you kill Mary Kate?" Tom came straight out with it.

"My, my! Give a dog a bad name. You won't believe, Tom, the number of women I'm meant to have raped and killed. And over so many countries and over such a long time. Alas, if only half of it were true." Fletcher sighed.

"Is that a yes or a no?" Tom persisted.

"Mmm. Let me see. Mary Kate. Ahh, yes, she brings back happy memories. Pretty little thing. So *ripe* for the taking." Fletcher smiled at him. He was thoroughly enjoying himself.

Tom had fully expected him to play games but could still feel the anger rise up inside him. He wasn't any good at disguising it, and Fletcher immediately picked up on it and his smile broadened.

"How did you get into the apartment?" Tom pushed on.

"How could I? Wasn't it all locked up, all safe and sound?"

It was now or never.

"I see. Thank you very much, Mr. Fletcher, for your time," Tom said as he started to gather up his papers.

Tom's tactics for this interview had been discussed at length. Tom knew he wouldn't be able to bully or cajole a confession out of him. The only way they would ever find out the truth would be if he decided to tell them. And the only way he would offer that up would be as something to gloat about, to show them how smart he was. But was Tom playing it right? Had he stopped too soon?

"Is that it?" inquired Fletcher, unsure where this was going. Ever since his old adversary had asked him to meet with Tom, he had contemplated how he was going to play him. He knew one thing for sure—he was really going to enjoy himself. But Tom had now thrown a curveball, and Fletcher couldn't quite work out the play.

"Yes, that's it," said Tom, putting on a lot more confidence than he was feeling. "I told them I thought that this meeting was a bad idea from the start. There is absolutely nothing to be gained from meeting you. No matter what you tell me, there's no way of telling whether it's the truth or not. So, at the end of the day, we'll be none the wiser. As far as I'm concerned, the crime will always remain unsolved." Tom kept up his appearance of calm as Fletcher seemed to be calling his bluff as he watched him close his briefcase. *Come on, please take the bait*, Tom screamed to himself as he put on his coat and walked towards the door.

"SIT DOWN!" Fletcher commanded as Tom reached for the handle.

Tom stalled for a second. He didn't want to appear too eager. He slowly turned around, looked at Fletcher and then returned to his chair.

"Arrogant assholes, they were. All three of them, thick as thieves," Fletcher said as he clasped his hands together and smiled at Tom.

"How did you get into the apartment?" Tom repeated his earlier question.

"Ah, the crux of the whole case. Maybe I just pressed the buzzer, and she let me in. What do you think?"

"I think not."

"Why? She was such a *sweetheart*. Maybe I gave her some sob story about running out of milk or something like that. Her being such a good neighbour and all."

"At three in the morning? No way. Do you know what I think?"

Fletcher didn't answer. He just shrugged his shoulders and smiled at Tom.

"I believe you had been stalking her for a while. You were probably the reason why she was so security conscious."

"I'll tell you, she was such a good looking lady. Who knows? If she had been nicer to me, maybe things would have worked out so differently for everybody. But NO, they thought they were so much better than me. Especially her. She deserved to die. Treated me like a piece of shit, she did. I asked her out three times. *Three fucking times* and the bitch didn't even have the manners to say no. Just kept on stringing me along, letting me think I had a chance.

209

But then, I realised she was only playing with me, fobbing me off with excuses. Well. She got what she deserved. And Jamie! And then the way it ended between him and Shane. Well, that was the real icing on the cake." Fletcher's piercing blue eyes stared through Tom, who instantly saw what this man was capable of.

Please God, don't let him stop now, Tom thought.

"Was she your first?"

"I suppose I should really thank her. She set me off on a glorious path."

"But she didn't let you in?" Tom held his breath.

"No."

Fletcher studied him.

"You had a key?" Tom finally came out with it.

A wry smile developed across Fletcher's face and then he clapped his hands slowly.

"Bravo. Bravo."

"She gave you a key?"

Fletcher just looked at him.

"Why would she give me a key?" he finally asked Tom.

"To let a tradesman in," Tom tried to suppress a smile, but couldn't.

"The apartments were relatively new at the time, and there were quite a few snagging problems. I think at some stage she asked you to let a workman in for her as she couldn't be there. You used that opportunity to get a copy cut. You were probably in and out of her apartment a lot. That's why she was so spooked. Maybe items of her clothing were going missing, and things were moved around."

"Close but no cigar, Mr. Dylan. You very nearly solved it. But I *swear* Mary Kate didn't give me a key."

Tom had prepared himself for his denial and was actually expecting it. But he knew Fletcher had chosen his words very carefully. More than likely, it was part of the game.

Fletcher had all but confirmed that he had had a key and

murdered Mary Kate. But Mary Kate hadn't given him the key.

"Who gave you the key?"

"Do you know justice has a funny way of coming to us all? The man responsible for the deaths of Mary Kate and Jamie is currently serving a lot of time over in your wee country." Fletcher was now in sheer ecstasy and laughed loudly as Tom struggled to take in the enormity of his statement.

"What? Who? Surely not Shane Bradley?" Tom asked incredulously.

"Priceless, isn't it? Man, when I heard what he did to Jamie, I pissed myself laughing. Yep, that big fucking oaf gave me a key. Mary Kate had asked him to let some workmen in while she was out, but they got delayed, and he had to pop out for about twenty minutes. He called me, and I was more than happy to help. Now me, I'd never pass up on a golden opportunity, so I got myself down quick smart to the cobbler around the corner and got myself the golden key. Had it for about four months before me and Mary Kate got our shit together."

Finally, the truth.

But how was he going to break the news to Shane?

"Why didn't Jamie go to help her? Was he that much out of it that he didn't wake up?"

"Yes. He was blind drunk and sleeping like a baby." The sinister smile told Tom there was more to come so he stayed quiet and waited for Fletcher to continue. Tom knew at this stage he wanted to tell the whole story.

"Besides, we really didn't make that much noise. She was a very quiet lover. She didn't even put up much of a struggle."

"Why not?" Tom asked but immediately regretted the question. By asking the question, it seemed to diminish in some way what he had done to Mary Kate. Fletcher was trying to imply that it was more like consensual sex rather than a brutal rape. Furthermore, Fletcher delighted in the question.

"I could tell she was a virgin. When we were in the middle of it, I could tell she was starting to enjoy herself. She…"

"Enough, you sick fuck."

Even though Tom had never met Mary Kate, he felt he had known her for over half his life. He wasn't going to have her memory besmirched in this way. He had gotten what he came for and didn't want to spend another moment in Fletcher's company. The man was pure evil. Tom was leaving this time, and there was no showboating about it.

But Fletcher was now on a roll.

"Oh, I forgot to mention that I told her if she woke him up, I would crack his skull wide open before coming back to finish her off. As I said, she was such a sweet girl, always thinking of others." Fletcher laughed in Tom's face.

"Fuck you. You rot in hell." Tom went to storm out of the room.

"Wait," Fletcher shouted after him. "Do you want to know her last words?"

Tom paused.

"After I finished with her, I was trying to decide what to do with her. She was my first. I wasn't as experienced then. I had decided the best option was to kill them both so I picked up the poker and was going to do him first. She was whimpering away in the corner, but she turned her head, and when she saw me about to batter him, she shouted, *Jamie. Jamie. No!* He wasn't making any noise or going anywhere so I reckoned I should do her first, shut the bitch up, you understand? After that, I was just about to bludgeon him when it came into my head—how about framing him? It was the perfect fit-up. Ingenious, don't you think?"

Chapter 41

SHANE SAT IMPATIENTLY in the Visitors Room of the Midlands prison waiting for Tom to arrive. He had spoken to him over the phone, but Tom wouldn't tell him anything. All he said was that he had critical information but would only tell him in person, and he would travel straight down from the airport. Shane had always hoped for closure but never believed it would come. He had nearly resigned himself to the fact that he would die without ever finding out the truth. Hopefully, the moment of truth was very near.

The door swung open and in walked a very glum looking Tom Dylan. He certainly didn't seem to be the bearer of good news. However, Tom was alone and this puzzled Shane. Where was Brannigan? The arrangement was that Brannigan would collect Tom at the airport and drive him to the prison.

"Where's Brannigan?" Shane asked.

"I told him I wasn't in a position to discuss anything with him until after I spoke to you first in private. He's eagerly waiting outside."

"Oh. How did he take that?"

"How do you think?" With that, both men laughed. It seemed

to ease the tension slightly.

"Well?" Shane looked at his old friend. "Was Brannigan's theory correct?"

"Sit down, Shane. Please." Tom didn't realise it, but he was trying to buy time. He had agonised since his meeting with Fletcher as to what exactly he was going to share with Shane. He was still undecided. After all, what did it matter who had given Fletcher the key? But could he really lie to Shane about this? This was the one thing that had consumed Shane Bradley's life since he murdered his best friend. No matter what the consequences, inevitably Shane deserved the whole truth?

Tom composed himself.

"Fletcher admitted it. He killed Mary Kate."

Shane let out a deep sigh and slowly nodded his head.

"So I slaughtered my best friend for something he didn't do," Shane whispered.

"You weren't to know, Shane. I genuinely believe that you weren't in control of your own mind when you did what you did. You were under such pressure."

"It still doesn't take away from the fact that I slaughtered him."

"Look, Shane, it was such a long time ago. You cannot go back and undo what's done. Please don't torture yourself about it. What's done is done. At least you've been finally able to clear Jamie's name. Isn't that what you wanted?"

"I wanted the truth. That's all I ever wanted. Jamie promised me the truth. He promised me that everything would work out. He promised me Mary Kate would live, that his God would look after it. I thought his confession was probably beaten out of him, and I pushed him on it. But he wouldn't budge, not even to me. I knew he was holding back on me. And then when Mary Kate died, and my Dad told me what she said at the very end, her pleading with him to stop, I just flipped."

Tom didn't say anything. In all the years he had known Shane, he had never once spoken about the night he killed Jamie. This was now his time. For his own sake, Shane desperately needed to unburden himself. Tom waited but said nothing.

"I hadn't intended to kill him, you know. I actually wasn't even going to hurt him. I know it all looked so pre-mediated with me drugging him and buying the petrol. But I only wanted to scare him, to get him to tell me the truth. But then Jamie looked like he was going to confess, I couldn't believe it. I totally panicked. I didn't want him to believe he would be absolved of his sins if he confessed them and asked for forgiveness. He had such a profound faith in God. And now it turns out that the poor man had nothing to do with it at all. He was as much a victim as Mary Kate." Shane put his head in his hands.

"As I said, Shane, you weren't to know. Please put it behind you."

Shane just sat there for a few moments when suddenly he bolted upright.

"How long was he there?" Shane shouted.

"What do you mean?"

"Was he already in her apartment waiting for her when I dropped her home that night?"

"Come on, Shane. What does that matter? Nobody could have known what was going to happen. Does it—"

"Tom, I need to know all the facts. Just give them to me. There's no reason to sugar-coat them. Please, Tom."

"I will, Shane, but please, bear in mind we only have his word for what happened that night. He's a real nasty piece of work so you can't take everything he says as gospel." Tom was trying to sow the seeds for later.

"Thanks, Tom. Duly noted, but was he waiting for her?"

"He says he was."

"The bastard. Did he say how long did he have a key?"

"Again, Shane, he said he got a key cut about four months previously."

215

"Four months! How he planned it for that long? Was he just waiting for the right opportunity?"

"He didn't say."

"And was Brannigan's theory correct? Had she given him a key to let a workman in?" Shane asked.

Tom chose his words carefully.

"Brannigan was correct. He was given a key temporarily to let the plumber in, but he immediately went off and got a key cut for himself."

Shane didn't appear to notice his subtle wording.

"What did he say about Jamie? Surely, no matter how drunk he was, he would have heard Mary Kate trying to fight him off?"

"That's the thing, Shane. Fletcher said he told Mary Kate he would kill Jamie if he came to so, according to him, Mary Kate didn't put up much resistance so that he wouldn't hurt Jamie. But after the rape, Fletcher decided he would kill them both. That's when Mary Kate shouted *Jamie. Jamie. No!* Fletcher was standing over him about to bludgeon him to death. Fletcher stopped and then went back over to Mary Kate." Tom paused briefly before continuing. "Jamie never woke up throughout the whole ordeal. That's why he couldn't remember. There was nothing for him to remember. He was passed out drunk the whole time. Fletcher then decided to frame Jamie."

"What a bastard."

"Yes, Shane. He's one evil son of a bitch. But at least we now know the truth and, if it's any consolation, Jamie was totally innocent," Tom concluded.

"Yes. And all because poor Mary Kate gave the wrong neighbour a key."

Tom gulped. He didn't know whether this was a statement or a question? Either way, he wasn't going to respond.

"But what does Mrs. Hamilton know? How does she know, or how did her husband know Jamie couldn't have done it?"

"We'll find out soon enough. I'll arrange that we meet her as

216

soon as possible. Now I better go and put Brannigan out of his misery. I'd say he's climbing the walls by now, what do you think?" Tom asked, but he could tell Shane didn't hear a word he said. He was deep in thought.

"Wait a minute, Tom. Did Fletcher say that it was actually her who gave him the key?"

Tom just looked at him but didn't answer.

"What if Mary Kate didn't give the key to him. In actual fact, it would have been most unlike her to part with a key. Maybe she had asked Jamie to wait for the plumber. When the plumber got delayed and didn't show up on time, maybe Jamie had to be somewhere else, perhaps attend a lecture in college or something like that, and he, in all innocence, gave the key to Fletcher."

Tom tried to defuse the nuclear bomb that was about to go off.

"What does it matter who gave him the key? People generally give their neighbours a key if they're stuck or away. It's a very regular event. Who could have known what was going to happen? Shane, it's totally irrelevant who gave Fletcher the key."

Tom hoped that this would put an end to the matter, but he very much doubted it.

"Yes, Tom, you're probably right. But what if it was Jamie who gave him the key, and Professor Hamilton somehow became aware of that fact. Christ, I'm so confused! That still doesn't explain how they could say that Jamie couldn't have done it. Did Fletcher say who gave him the key?"

Tom Dylan took a deep breath.

Chapter 42

NED BRANNIGAN WAS worried. He would now have the financial resources to do whatever he wished for the rest of his life. But that didn't give him much comfort if he had to spend the next ten years or so rotting in an Irish prison.

He was sitting in an O'Brien's sandwich shop he had come across which was only about seven hundred metres away from Mary Kate's old apartment. Again, for the umpteenth time, he studied the report that Tom had prepared to detail his meeting with Fletcher. He had insisted that Tom type it up and not to leave anything out, no matter how insignificant it appeared. It wasn't a very big report, just twenty-three pages in total, but it was extremely comprehensive. Ned was sure he was missing something. The initial hysteria over finally cracking the case was now gone, and what was he left with? Nothing. Okay, the case was solved, and it would make him an extremely wealthy man, but it didn't get him out of his current predicament. All in all, Brannigan knew the only way to guarantee his freedom would be to expose the fact that the guards were involved in a cover up and that they knew they had the wrong man. In actual fact, he thought he mightn't necessarily have to bring the cover up into the public domain. He was convinced that Cullen would back down and drop the charges if he thought Brannigan could prove the cover-up.

But it wasn't there. There was nothing that even hinted at such a cover up. Before Tom met Fletcher, all he could actually prove was that Fletcher couldn't have seen Mary Kate and Jamie as he said he had from the window as he walked by her apartment. Now, all he had was the confession of a convicted psychopathic murderer. No, he didn't even have that. All he had was the word of Shane Bradley's long-term friend and solicitor that a serial killer had confessed to him. Furthermore, there was no audio recording or any other witness to confirm the validity of the confession. Big O had enough for his blockbuster movie, now complete with the ending. But that was it. More than likely, Fletcher would play his games and repudiate Tom's testimony. Who knows, Fletcher may even sue!

Brannigan also felt very stupid and naive. Earlier that day he had reached out to Big O for help. "Trust me, Ned. I'll move heaven and earth for you. You're like a brother to me, man. Cullen isn't going to get away with it. I have friends in very high places who owe me. You're not alone on this one. We'll get you back home soon. Hang in there, man. Trust me, okay?"

"Sure thing, Big O."

But he wasn't sure at all. Ned certainly didn't trust him, and he knew that he was now expendable. He also suspected Big O was pondering whether it might be a good thing for the movie if Ned actually went to jail. It would definitely give the film a lot more publicity, even maybe a focus point.

Ned was now very much on his own.

"Would you care for a refill, sir?"

The waiter interrupted his thoughts.

"Yes, please," Brannigan replied without even lifting his head.

"Glorious day, thank God," the waiter continued.

Christ, what is it with the Irish and their Cead Mile Failte. The last thing he needed right now was small talk. Or maybe, on

220

second thought, it was exactly what he needed. A break would do him good. Brannigan decided to engage and dropped Tom's report.

"Yes, it is," Brannigan replied and made eye contact with the young man.

Like a true professional, he immediately seized on Brannigan's accent.

"Do you mind if I ask you what part of the States you're from?"

"LA."

"And are you over here on holiday or on business?"

Brannigan laughed.

"Well, initially, it was business, but now it's turned into an extended holiday."

"Very good. Well, I hope you enjoy your stay. Is there anything else I can get you, sir?" He was polished all right. He knew the Americans liked to be addressed with respect.

"No thanks. How's business going, anyway? It seemed a bit quiet today," Brannigan asked, more to keep the conversation going than anything else. He was starting to dread the thoughts of returning to that bloody report again.

"Ah, sure, you get days like this. But overall, we've been very lucky since we took on the O'Brien's franchise."

"Oh, and when did you change?"

"Coming up to three years now. The building has been in my family since it was built. My father used to run a successful dry-cleaner from here, but things started to go downhill fast when the recession hit. Believe me, it took a lot of persuading a few years back to get him to close the dry-cleaners and take out the franchise. We haven't looked back since."

"Good for you, kid. So do you own it now?"

He hesitated briefly before answering.

"Yes. I own it now. I love to come out and actually meet the customers."

"Well, best of luck with it. Thanks for the refill," Brannigan said to terminate the conversation and reluctantly returned to the report again.

"You're welcome, sir. Enjoy your day." He knew when not to impose on customers and duly took the hint.

Christ. Brannigan had nearly missed it.

"Wait. Wait. Come back," he shouted after him.

The owner was startled by the urgency in his voice and immediately thought something was wrong.

"Yes, sir. Is everything okay?" he asked nervously.

"Yes, yes, yes. There's something you might be able to help me with," Brannigan said as he grabbed Tom's report and began frantically flicking through the pages.

"Yes, here it is," he proclaimed and then proceeded to read the relevant section aloud.

"...he said that he 'couldn't look a gift horse in the mouth' and he immediately went to a local cobbler to get a key cut."

Brannigan couldn't contain his excitement.

"And then, in brackets afterwards, Dylan goes on to say, *Cobblers in Ireland back then not only mended shoes, but they also provided a key cutting service. They normally traded out of a dry-cleaners."* Brannigan finished with a flourish and looked up at a bewildered young man, who hadn't a clue what was going on.

"So?"

"I'm really sorry, sir, but I don't fully understand what you're asking me?"

"Was there also a cobbler in the dry-cleaners?"

"Yes."

"And did you provide a key-cutting service?"

"Oh, yes. Yes, we did. Of course. It was actually quite a lucrative part—"

"I need to meet with your father straight away. Can you call him now?"

The young man looked down at the floor.

"I'm afraid that won't be possible. He died tragically last

month."

"Oh. I'm sorry to hear that. Do you mind me asking what happened?"

"He was killed in a hit-and-run accident," the young man replied solemnly.

Brannigan was stunned. *My God, could it be?*

Surely not. It was pure coincidence. But Brannigan didn't believe in coincidences. How far would Cullen go? He didn't even know yet whether that man had any connection with the case, but he decided then and there he wasn't going to wait to find out.

It was time to put Plan B into operation.

Time to run.

He had contemplated it before. It was actually very easy. He would have no problem losing the tail that followed him everywhere. Then, just jump on a ferry over to Britain, no passport required for that. Once he was in Britain, he'd get his contacts to kick in and get a false passport. He wouldn't risk flying directly to the States, maybe Canada or Mexico, and then he'd cross back into the safety of his own country. Once he was at home, he was very confident Cullen wouldn't pursue an extradition. If he did, bring it on. He was a US citizen, and Cullen would have some fight on his hands.

"What did you want to talk to my dad about? And what did you mean when you said he said he couldn't look a gift horse in the mouth?"

"Oh, nothing. Never mind. It's just some old case I'm working on. Thank you. You've been most helpful."

"It wouldn't happen to be the Mary Kate Quinn murder case, would it? You know, that actually took place very near here. You just go up—"

"Yes, I know," Brannigan cut him off. His mind was racing, and he now wanted time on his own.

"Sorry. I'll leave you to it, but that's so weird. That case really bugged my dad. He was convinced that the young lad—I think

Jamie Ryan was his name—anyway, he was convinced that he was innocent. He even came forward and made a statement to the guards at that time."

Brannigan's ears pricked up. He knew Dylan's defence file like the back of his hand. The prosecution was duty bound to give the defence everything they had, and that included all statements the guards had taken, even if the guards deemed the statements to have no relevance to the case. Most of the statements were from people at the twenty-first party, but he couldn't recall any statement in Jamie's favour.

"Really. Listen, I'm sorry to intrude, but would it be possible for you to give me five minutes of your time." Brannigan was always able to turn on the charm when he wanted to.

"Yes. Sure. We're not that busy at the moment. Sarah—" he called up to the young girl behind the counter "—can you keep an eye on things for a few minutes. I'm just going to have a chat over here. Thanks."

He sat down opposite Brannigan.

"I'm sorry. Where are my manners? Ned Brannigan's the name," he said as he offered his hand.

"Peter Molloy," the young man replied and shook his hand.

"Thanks, Peter, for your time. Now, tell me, do you know why your father was convinced Jamie Ryan was innocent?"

"Well, my dad remembered dealing with a man a few months before the murder. He said he couldn't forget this guy because of what he did. Dad said he rushed in and demanded to get a key cut there and then. Dad casually told him to call back in about an hour or so, as he had a backlog to do and also the dry-cleaners happened to be very busy that day. At this stage, the man got quite aggressive and grabbed my father. He told him he needed the key cut now, and he wasn't going to take no for an answer. Now, Ned, my father was a big man and didn't scare easily, but he said there was something really sinister about the fellow. Dad was deciding what to do when the man, while still holding Dad with one hand,

224

reached into his pocket and threw an old ten-punt note on the counter."

"So your father cut the key for him?" Brannigan asked.

"Well, the way Dad saw it, it gave him an out. At that stage, it cost twenty pence to get a key cut, and also Dad wanted this guy out of the shop. So, yes, he jumped him up to the top of the queue and cut the key for him then and there."

"I see. But how did that lead him to make a statement to the guards in the Mary Kate murder?"

"Dad didn't think any more of it at the time. But then one day, he's sitting down watching the news on TV, and who does he see, but the man."

"The guy who threatened him? The man who got the key cut?"
"Yes."

"On the news! What was he on the news for?"

"Well, it was the news item about the attack on Mary Kate. It turns out that he's a neighbour of hers, and he's telling the world how nice a lady she is, and he hopes that she'll pull through. He was only ever in one news clip, the six o'clock one. He was cut for the nine o'clock."

"Wow! Then what did your father do?"

"He immediately rang the guards and told them that he might have some evidence in relation to the case. He said he wasn't sure if it had any bearing on the case, but they could decide that. They told him that they would be back in contact in due course and, sure enough, a few days later, two young guards came and took his statement."

"And that was the end of it, yeah?"

"No. Dad thought it was. But, about a week or so later, after that young Ryan fella was charged, one of the detectives investigating the case called around to Dad and went through everything with him in great detail. Dad actually felt the guard was trying to confuse him. Showing him mug shots and trying to get him to pick out the man. Dad said the man wasn't in any of the mug shots. Eventually, he thanked Dad for his help, but told him they had fully investigated the matter, and the neighbour wasn't connected in any way with the case. But Dad wasn't convinced, and he told the Detective so."

"How did that go down?"

"Not very well, actually. Dad said he got quite angry and told him that they knew what they were doing and that Jamie Ryan had already confessed. He repeated that they had followed up the lead, as they had done with every lead, and it had proved to be entirely innocent. But Dad persisted, and that's when it got ugly."

"Ugly? What do you mean?"

"Well, ugly is probably the wrong word. The guard turned very nasty. He said the matter was closed, and he didn't want to hear another word about it. That's when he threatened my father."

"Threatened him. In what way?"

"He ordered him not to discuss this matter again with anybody. Then, Dad said, he put his face into his and warned him that he didn't want him as an enemy and to drop it. Well, my dad was totally taken aback. I mean, he was only trying to help and—"

"Yes, I know. Deplorable behaviour," Brannigan said, knowing too well he had done the same on more than one occasion when he was a cop. Well-intentioned people can sometimes fuck up a case. "Tell me, Peter, what did your Dad do?"

"He heeded his advice."

Clever man, thought Brannigan. Sometimes he wished he had done the same.

"My father could actually see the detective's point of view. After all, the detective said that Ryan had confessed, and they had investigated the matter that he had brought to their attention. He didn't want anything to confuse the issue. All the same, though, it really bothered him that he had actually threatened him."

"Thanks, Peter. I've just two more quick questions if you don't mind?"

"Not at all."

"First, what was your father's name?"

"Andrew Molloy."

Brannigan was now absolutely certain his statement wasn't in Dylan's file. He never forgot a name and, although he would double-check the file again, he knew the statement wouldn't be there."

"And secondly, and most importantly, by any chance, you wouldn't happen to know the name of the detective who came to see your father, the detective who threatened him."

Brannigan held his breath and hoped.

"As a matter of fact, I would. Would you believe he's now actually the highest-ranking guard in the country, Commissioner Cullen?"

Game. Set. And match.

Chapter 43

SITTING IN HER parlour, Mrs. Hamilton stared intently at Shane Bradley as Tom Dylan explained in detail once again the actual facts behind the murder of Mary Kate. But Mrs. Hamilton was suspicious and remained unconvinced.

"Mr. Dylan, you say that this man Fletcher was a neighbour of Mary Kate's, and then you go on to say that Mary Kate was his first victim. Yet, you also say he was in Ireland at that time under a false identity. Why would he need to use a false identity if Mary Kate was his first? Well? Please answer me that, Mr. Dylan," she sat back smugly.

"You're totally correct in what you say, Mrs. Hamilton. As I stated, Mary Kate was the first woman he ever raped and murdered. He went on to kill many others. But he had originally fled to Ireland because he was up on charges relating to a very serious assault in Manchester. He was involved in a fight outside a pub where the other man ended up losing an eye."

"I see. I presume, Mr. Dylan, that Fletcher was good enough to provide you with a written statement admitting his guilt?" she continued. It was as if she hadn't heard him at all.

"He didn't, ma'am." Dylan didn't like where this was going.

"You must remember that he's a ruthless, cold-blooded killer who—"

"So you said, Mr. Dylan. I may be old, but there is nothing wrong with my hearing," she cut across him sternly.

"I'm sorry, Mrs. Hamilton. I didn't mean to imply—"

"And you say it was as simple as that. He was given a key to let a workman in, and the scoundrel took advantage and had a key cut for himself. And you say this happened a few months before he actually struck. So, he had a key cut and waited a few months before he attacked! Doesn't sound like a cold-blooded killer to me!"

"That's what he told me, Mrs. Hamilton."

"Okay. And I presume you had witnesses to this conversation? Don't dare tell me you were stupid enough to meet him on your own, and there's nobody to collaborate your story. Tell me, Mr. Dylan, who was with you at that meeting?"

At this stage, Tom was utterly crestfallen. He knew that she was a tough woman. But he thought she would have been delighted to finally learn the truth and might thaw out a little. But he was now very much on the back foot, and he really wasn't sure if he, no they, would be able to convince her to tell them what she knew.

"I did meet him by myself, Mrs. Hamilton. I took a calculated risk. The way I saw it, I thought the best chance of him telling me the truth was to have a one to one conversation with him. You see, he's—"

"That's so convenient, Mr. Dylan. So, let me get this clear in my mind. Without reviewing the photos myself, I understand from you that there were doubts cast over the validity of certain evidence. But, as things stand, all I have is a story that you met a convicted murderer in Britain who told you that he killed Mary Kate and then, rather than killing Jamie Ryan, decided to frame him. That you—"

"No, Mrs. Hamilton, you have a lot more than that," Tom exploded. "You have my word."

Her mouth opened again to speak, but no words came out. She was a woman of honour. Her word was her bond. And she recognised the same character in Tom Dylan. Was it time to tell? To finally let go? She only now realised she had carried the secret for so long that it felt like an act of betrayal giving it up. But it was time for closure, for all their sakes.

"Very well, Mr. Dylan. I believe you." Finally, the thaw.

"Mr. Bradley. I gather that you and Jamie Ryan were the best of friends. Was that so?" She was actually quite civil to him, which caught him a bit by surprise.

"Yes. We were very close, as close as you could get," Shane answered.

"I see. And did he ever mention to you that he was a patient of my late husband?"

"No, he didn't, but it was such a long time ago." Shane glanced over at Tom and then continued. "No. I'm certain he didn't. If he had, I'm sure I would remember something like that."

"Just as I thought. And, generally speaking, as best friends would you have been his closest confidante?"

"Yes, absolutely."

"So does it strike you as strange that he never once mentioned it?"

"Yes. I'm genuinely amazed. We were so close. We discussed everything together. I didn't think we had secrets from each other. Why wouldn't he tell me he was seeing a doctor?"

"Exactly as I suspected" Mrs. Hamilton sighed but then, in a split second, her sigh turned to anger. "What a silly, silly boy. All this pain, this suffering, it could so easily have been avoided. And to think how many lives ruined by his stupidity. His own life so brutally destroyed, your life too, Mr. Bradley, ruined. And not to mention my poor, tormented Godfrey. And me, Mr. Bradley, my life too." She now turned towards Tom.

"And you say this man Fletcher went on to kill many more women. How disastrous. He could have saved all those women.

231

How stupid."

Tom and Shane didn't even dare breathe.

Mrs. Hamilton stood up.

"Very well, Mr. Bradley. I promised you the truth. Jamie Ryan was a patient of my husband, Professor Godfrey Hamilton. My husband was an Endocrinologist, which meant he specialised in Endocrinology." She looked at both of them and realised she had lost them already.

"I'll try to keep this as simple as I can. In layman's terms, Godfrey specialised in glands. Now one of the most important glands in the human body is the pituitary gland. It has many functions, many essential ones, but one of its functions is the production of testosterone. Do either of you know what testosterone is?"

Shane decided to be brave enough and ventured an answer.

"I think so. Isn't that what athletes take to make them stronger, to give them more strength and stamina?"

Mrs. Hamilton threw her eyes up to heaven, but then, surprisingly, smiled at him.

"I suppose not a bad attempt. It is actually the primary male sex hormone. Jamie Ryan was referred by his local doctor to my husband because he had very low testosterone levels and—"

"Are you sure? It doesn't sound like—"

"Please, Mr. Bradley." Mrs. Hamilton then paused before continuing. "Please, Shane, don't interrupt me. I know you're very eager to hear everything. I'll explain it all to you to the best of my ability and afterwards, I promise I'll answer all your questions. Is that okay?" She smiled at him again.

Shane was beginning to warm to this withered old woman and nodded a reply.

"Okay. Thank you. As I said, my husband was one of the leading experts in Ireland on the pituitary gland and, by extension, testosterone. He did some blood tests which confirmed that Jamie did indeed have quite a low level. Fortunately, the condition is extremely treatable, and Godfrey set about his work. Jamie wasn't long into his treatment when Mary Kate was murdered."

She paused and then took a sip of water.

"When Godfrey heard that Jamie Ryan was charged with rape—initially that was the charge—he was deeply perplexed by it. Jamie had struck him as such a sweet kid—a very pleasant young man was how Godfrey described him. Godfrey didn't think it was in his nature to commit such a crime. But one never knows, does one? But, more importantly, he didn't believe, given the particular circumstances of the case, that Jamie Ryan was physically capable of the crime."

"Sweet Jesus," Tom exclaimed.

"You mean physically, he wasn't capable of rape? Then why—"

"Silence. Silence, I say," Mrs. Hamilton roared.

"Please, let me continue, and you may ask your questions later," she composed herself.

"Jamie was certainly capable of the physical crime of rape, in as much as he was able to maintain an erection. But the reason he went to his general practitioner and then to Godfrey was because of his medical condition—he wasn't capable of ejaculation. At that stage, his testosterone levels were too low. Godfrey read a newspaper article written at that time in relation to new technology that they were trying to develop that would help solve such crimes. Nowadays, DNA analysis and semen analysis are invaluable in the solving of crime, but back then, the science was only in its infancy. However, this article said that the guards were now preserving semen found in rape cases in the hope that maybe one day the technology would be able to help them. The article specifically mentioned Mary Kate's case, and that's when Godfrey knew that Jamie Ryan couldn't have done it."

Stunned silence

"Would either of you two gentlemen care to join me?" she said as she stifled back a tear. It wasn't a request. It was an order. She produced a bottle of Cognac and proceeded to pour three large glasses. She then resumed sitting.

Tom was first to speak. "It doesn't make any sense. Why wouldn't Jamie have just told the guards? Pure madness. He knew he couldn't have done it! What's more, he could have proved it, but chose not to. Why would he do such a stupid thing?"

"Initially, Jamie wasn't one hundred percent sure that he couldn't have done it. Godfrey had commenced his treatment, and his testosterone levels were rising. When he was out on bail, he went to see Godfrey and asked him if it was possible that he could commit such a crime. He told Godfrey that he couldn't remember what happened that night. Godfrey assured him it was impossible, he couldn't have done it. Godfrey suggested that they go to the guards together, and Godfrey would clear the matter up. He said Jamie seemed very unsure, and Godfrey pushed him on it. That's when Jamie told him no. He said that Mary Kate's life was in God's hands and, by his actions or inactions, he could save her. It was all a test, he told Godfrey, and they had to trust in the Lord. Jamie said it was the only way to save her life. Godfrey argued with him, but to no avail. His mind was set, and he was not for turning."

"Why did your husband send me the notes? Why didn't he just go to the guards himself?" Tom asked.

"Godfrey was going to do that and told Jamie so. He told Jamie that he was under tremendous stress and probably didn't realise it. The stress was causing him to think irrationally. Godfrey told him he simply couldn't respect his wishes. He told Jamie his plan was insane, and he was going to go to the guards himself. But Jamie got extremely angry. He told my husband he had to remember his Hippocratic Oath—he was not at liberty to discuss doctor/patient information with anybody. He was the patient and he forbade it and—"

"And your husband bought that?" Shane shouted. "What sort of a man was he? He let an innocent man die and—"

"No, Mr. Bradley, he did not. Nobody knew what you were going to do. You killed Jamie Ryan. You alone did it, and nobody else. I am quite sure if the case had come to trial, Godfrey would have stepped forward. But, because of your actions, we will never know. Don't you dare try to blame my husband—your hand, and your hand only, Mr. Bradley."

Everybody paused for breath.

"I think we're all very emotional at the minute, and it might be a good idea if we all calmed down," Tom finally said as he indulged himself and took a large swig of his drink. Never in his wildest dreams was he expecting what he had just heard. It defied logic. Tom thought back to his meetings with Jamie, to the fire in his eyes, his iron stubbornness, his constant calling on higher powers to make things right.

Shane and Mrs. Hamilton looked at each other, and Mrs. Hamilton slowly nodded.

"Okay. So, let me get this straight. Jamie Ryan had a medical condition which meant he was incapable of ejaculation, and because there was semen found at the scene, he then knew he was an innocent man. Only two people had this knowledge, Jamie and his physician, your late husband, Professor Hamilton. However, because of some twisted religious belief, Jamie convinced himself that the only way to save Mary Kate's life was to pass some bizarre test from God, which… I'm getting myself confused right now," Tom trailed off.

Shane took up the running.

"The test was simply to put his total faith in God. God would show mercy if Jamie passed the test. Mary Kate would be spared, and then she would be able to reveal the truth and prove Jamie's innocence."

"As I said, my husband did question Jamie's sanity. But, you also have to remember, the case never came to trial." Her eyes wandered over to Shane. "So the boy could have produced the evidence to save himself at any time he wanted."

"Such absolute twisted logic! Unbelievable. Tell me, Mrs. Hamilton, did Jamie ever tell your husband why he confessed to a crime that he knew he couldn't have committed?" Tom asked.

"He had signed the confession while in police custody and before he was able to confirm with Godfrey that he was innocent. Godfrey did ask him how he could have signed such a confession when he knew there was a very strong possibility that he didn't do it. He told Godfrey that his time in Garda custody wasn't exactly a bed of roses, and they didn't believe him when he told them that he couldn't remember. Godfrey said he had options, and he could tell the court that the confession was made under duress. Armed with Godfrey's medical evidence, the court would have no choice but to believe him. But again, Jamie was having none of it and reverted to his belief that it was all a test from God that he must pass to save Mary Kate. It drove Godfrey to distraction."

"Did he say anything more about his time in Garda custody?" Shane followed up.

"Not that I am aware of. Although I do recall, years later, that one of the detectives on the case—Flood I think his name was—was actually dismissed from the force for police brutality. He was said to have been a member of The Heavy Gang. You've heard of The Heavy Gang, haven't you?"

"Yes. I think so. Weren't they a group of guards back in the seventies who didn't play by the book? They regularly beat suspects. But I thought they were mainly associated with the troubles and Republican prisoners?" Tom said.

"Possibly, but I firmly believe that the guards thought they had their man and beat the confession out of him. The checks and balances that apply in today's society were non-existent back then. You were his solicitor then. What is your opinion?" Mrs. Hamilton asked.

"I totally agree with you, and I've heard that allegation about Flood. I remember vividly that Jamie actually laughed when we reviewed the custody sergeant's records of his detention. I wanted to put the guards on the stand, to see if they might let something slip, but Jamie wouldn't hear of it. He never mentioned your husband but said the jury wouldn't take his word over a number of high-ranking guards, although he wasn't particularly concerned about the preparation of the case."

"I suppose going back to his idiotic strategy of putting his trust in God," Shane said, rolling his eyes to heaven.

The other two nodded slowly.

"I've just one or two more questions, if I may, Mrs. Hamilton? If your husband couldn't come forward, why then did he send me those notes?" Tom asked.

"He was trying to prod Jamie to tell you. Godfrey was extremely uncomfortable with the position he found himself in. He fretted about it constantly. He was genuinely worried that he could face prosecution for withholding evidence. He was also very upset at seeing the devastating effect that it was having on Jamie's family, especially his poor mother..."— again a lethal glance at Shane— "so he was hoping the notes would force Jamie's hand, so to speak."

"Jesus, why didn't he tell me?" said Shane. "I just can't understand it. We didn't have secrets. We told each other everything. Why didn't he just tell me he had a medical condition? He would have known I would have helped him."

"Pride, embarrassment, stupidity! Who knows," Mrs. Hamilton replied. "Men aren't very good at sharing things, Shane, and he was so young. Maybe he just wanted to handle it by himself."

Tom noticed it immediately, but it slipped by Shane. The tell was there. She was lying. She had suddenly avoided any eye contact and seemed to cut short her sentence. What was she hiding? Tom's legal training kicked in, and he went in search of the truth.

"Was he born with the medical condition?" Tom sat upright in his seat.

"Pardon?" she replied, but she then moved uncomfortably in her seat. She was stalling. Why?

"He... I don't know," and she reached out and grabbed her drink.

Many a night she had sat down beside the fire looking at her husband in a drunken stupor and dreaming of this moment. It had taken all her strength not to reveal all when they first met. But now that the moment had finally arrived, she was overawed by it. She thought that it would give her great satisfaction and, in some ways, would finally liberate her. In actual fact, she now thought it would only compound matters.

"Was he born with it?" Tom asked again, puzzled by her demeanour.

He has a right to know, she told herself. But all of a sudden, she felt pity whereas she was expecting anger.

She took a very deep breath.

"No. He wasn't born with the medical condition. The deficiency of the pituitary gland was as a direct result of blunt force trauma to the head," she replied as coolly and calmly as she could.

"What do you mean? An old rugby injury or something like that," Shane jumped in.

She hesitated again. She couldn't go through with it. For God's sake, he was only a child when it happened. He hadn't meant to inflict the damage that he had. Nobody could have possibly foreseen the consequences of his actions.

Shane reached out and tenderly touched her hand.

"Please tell me, Mrs. Hamilton. I have to know. I find it absolutely shocking that he kept this from me. It was just so unlike him. Please, Mrs. Hamilton, I have to know the truth."

"Very well, then, Mr. Bradley." She composed herself. So be it. "But first, you must answer *me* one question, something that baffled Godfrey and me for years."

"I certainly will if I can."

"After Mary Kate died, why didn't Jamie then come clean with you and tell you the truth, or as Godfrey would often say, why then didn't he play his Trump Card?"

"To be totally honest with you, Mrs. Hamilton, a lot of that day is a blur. Don't get me wrong—I know what I did, and I'm not trying to make any excuses for my deeds. Initially, I wasn't sure what I was going to do. I was devastated when Mary Kate died. We both were. He had me convinced that his God would save her. But I always felt he was holding back on me somehow, and I had to find out. He was my best friend. I had put everything on the line for him. The detective on the case, Cullen, had told me that he had previously attacked his former girlfriend, so I started to think that maybe he could have done it after all. I had only intended to frighten him, but then Jamie started saying he would tell me everything. I was sure he was about to confess. With Jamie's deep religious beliefs, that meant absolution, and I wasn't going to grant him that privilege. I flipped and did what I did."

The tears were now rolling down both cheeks.

"How wrong you were. I think he was going to tell you something else, something he had been trying to protect you from. From the scarring on the pituitary gland, Godfrey could tell that the injury was sustained a number of years earlier. It would have had to be a very forceful blow to cause such an injury, and Godfrey asked him could he remember such an incident. Godfrey told him it was highly likely that he would have lost consciousness for a time. Jamie told Godfrey about the incident that occurred the first time he met his best friend."

Mrs. Hamilton was now also in tears.

"Jamie Ryan didn't confide in you about his medical condition because he didn't want you to feel guilty. You caused his injury, Mr. Bradley."

Chapter 44

ONCE MORE UNTO the breach.

Tom was waiting for over fifty minutes, and nobody had bothered to even offer him a cup of coffee. Still, what else did he expect?

"Commissioner Cullen is ready to see you now. Please follow me," the young receptionist said as she led him down a narrow corridor to the Commissioner's office. She knocked on the door and waited patiently until he told her to enter. She announced Tom's arrival, ushered him in, and then left the room. They were now alone.

"Thank you for agreeing to meet me. I appreciate you're a very busy man," Tom said as he offered his hand. Cullen ignored it and gestured towards the seat opposite him.

Arrogant prat, thought Tom.

"Let's dispense with the formalities, shall we, Tom? You mentioned on the phone something about a man called Ned Brannigan and certain information that I needed to know. It was very much in my interest to meet you, you said. Well, let's hear it. You have five minutes."

"Okay. In relation to Jamie Ryan's case—"

"Shut up. Stand up," Cullen commanded.

"I beg your pardon?"

"You heard me. Just do it," Cullen repeated. He was now standing in front of Tom.

As Tom stood up, Cullen immediately grabbed him by the crotch. Tom was just about to push him away when Cullen proceeded to pat him down.

"Just making sure this is a private conversation. You understand, don't you?" He then pulled out a small electronic device out of a desk drawer and scanned Tom and his briefcase. No bugs.

Tom breathed a sigh of relief. Initially, Brannigan had wanted him to go with a wire, but Tom had refused, insisting it had to be done by the book. He had anticipated that Cullen would be extremely cautious and treat the whole meeting as a set-up.

"Okay, you're clean. Start talking."

"We have proof that Jamie Ryan didn't murder Mary Kate and, what's more, we also know that you personally know that. You've known that for years and—"

"You enjoy your trip to Strangeways? How is Fletcher keeping? That fucking murdering scumbag would say anything to show us upstanding cops in a bad light." Cullen smiled.

Tom was momentarily taken aback. Could he have been under surveillance because of his association with Brannigan? Brannigan had told him to be prepared for anything. Cullen would have done his homework before meeting him.

"Look, Commissioner. I don't want to be here any more than you do. I'm here to deliver a message—"

"Well, what's stopping you?"

"We know you were personally involved in beating a confession out of an innocent man— sorry, an innocent child—and you were then involved in a cover-up when you realised you had the wrong man."

"Careful with your words, boy. They could get you into

trouble."

"You don't scare me. You have blood on your hands. Christ, if you had acted when you realised you'd made a mistake, you could have saved a lot of women, not to mention Jamie Ryan."

"Watch yourself, Dylan. You're playing with the big boys now. You could get hurt."

"What? Like Andrew Molloy did recently. Is that what you mean? An old man ploughed down, and what was his crime? Trying to do his civic duty and help the guards? Or was it that he knew too much?"

Cullen glared at him, his red face looking as if it would explode out of his starched collar. Finally, he spoke.

"I'll give you this one for free. Andrew Molloy's death had nothing to do with me. You got that. And we'll catch the cowardly little bastards who drove off. Now, Tom, I presume you didn't come here to threaten me, did you?" Cullen was moving him on. What was the deal?

"No. Right. As I said, I'm here to deliver a message. A message from Ned Brannigan. Mr. Brannigan got what he came to Ireland for and would like to return to the States. You see, at the moment, he can't because he is facing charges of membership of an illegal organisation. Now, the way Mr. Brannigan sees it, he has two choices. His first choice is to go to the media and share everything we now know about the Jamie Ryan case—the botched Garda investigation, the beaten confession, the murderer under your very nose, allowed to skip off, murdering more innocent women because of your arrogance. All of this leading to the trumped-up charges he now faces—a picture of corruption that goes to the very top of the guards. Are you following me?" Tom was in now in full flow. Cullen didn't answer.

"Mr. Brannigan feels that once this is all out in the public domain, there's no chance of his case ever going to trial, and even if it did, there is no way there would be a conviction."

"And his second option?" Cullen asked slowly.

"As I said, he's gotten what he came for, and simply wants to go home. If the charges are dropped, Mr. Brannigan doesn't see any need for everyone's dirty laundry to be washed in public. He already has a great story, in that the crime is finally solved. How were the guards to know? After all, they had a signed confession from the man who was found lying beside her in a locked apartment. The story might focus on Jamie's religious beliefs, on his deluded faith that God would save Mary Kate." Tom smiled at him, but inside, he wanted to reach over and grab Cullen by the throat.

Cullen was about to ask a question but then thought better of it.

"I see, Mr. Dylan. You seem to be under the impression that I have some personal knowledge in relation to Mr. Brannigan's case. Let me state categorically, and for the record, I do not," Cullen said just in case he missed something. "If Mr. Brannigan is facing Anti-Terrorist charges, it's the responsibility of the ATU, and I'm sure you, as a practising solicitor, are fully aware that I cannot interfere in any way in a Garda investigation. In fact, Mr. Dylan, I am surprised and shocked at your conduct here today, and I may very well take this matter further. Good day to you," Cullen finished, dismissing him. He picked up some notes close to hand and pretended to read them.

No surprises then. The encounter went pretty much as expected.

"Thank you for your time," Tom said and departed, leaving his card on Cullen's desk.

Now the waiting game commenced. Would he take the bait?

Cullen sat there at his desk, scratching his head vigorously. Of all the cases to come back and haunt him, the Jamie Ryan one was the least he would have expected. Sure, he had bent the rules a little, but hadn't he got results? Now, he was in a jam, and he had to consider his options carefully. If he were honest with himself, he knew there was only one option, and even that wasn't great.

Somehow, these troublemakers had unravelled the case, and no matter what way he played it in his mind, the outcome for him wasn't good.

He would take Brannigan's deal. In fact, he had already been having second thoughts about letting Brannigan's case actually go to trial. There was too much heat associated with it. But he had enjoyed putting Brannigan on ice, and he reckoned he could have stalled the case for well over eighteen months or more. Brannigan would have to stay put, and he could keep a good eye on him. There was one problem with the deal—he didn't trust Brannigan. There was nothing to stop him reneging on it once he got Stateside.

"FUCK IT ANYWAY," he roared as he kicked a hole in his desk. He grabbed his landline and dialled Tom Dylan's mobile.

"Tom Dylan here." They were all on tenterhooks.

"How do I know he won't welch on the deal once he's a free man?"

"He'll sign whatever papers you need."

"Sign a piece of paper! That won't matter a fuck when he's back home in the States. I'm telling you, Dylan, I'm holding you personally responsible if he doesn't follow through. *Do you understand me?*" Cullen screamed and slammed down the phone.

They all looked at each other. Not enough, not by a long shot. No names were even mentioned. *Please don't let him leave the building and deliver the message in person.* If he did, the game was over.

Luckily, they didn't have to wait too long. Forty-two minutes after Tom left his office, Cullen made the fatal mistake. He speed dialled the number from his landline and, within seconds, spoke to the Head of the ATU.

"Hi, John. You know that favour you're doing for me, the yank Ned Brannigan?"

"Sure. Why? What's up?"

"I'm going to have to cut the bastard loose."

"You sure?"

"Yes, it breaks my heart, but let it go, drop all charges."

"Probably the right decision, boss. You know how the Americans are about their citizens, and I heard he has friends in high places. I've been getting a bit of heat about him, but nothing major. We'd have had to get our judge onside to see it through properly. Do you want me to fix him with anything else, maybe call some of the others and hit him with a drug charge or something like that? A two-to-five year sentence."

"Christ, John, don't tempt me." Cullen laughed. "No. Let him go. Drop all charges."

"Okay, boss. Well, look, at least we gave him a bloody nose and let him enjoy our Irish hospitality for a while. What did he do anyway?"

"Goodbye, John. Thanks again." Cullen hung up.

The Garda Ombudsman gave the order as he took off his headset.

Dylan and Brannigan had had a massive row a few days previously, but Dylan insisted it was the only route to go. Brannigan was sceptical when Dylan explained that the Ombudsman was independent of the guards and that it was their duty to investigate complaints against the Gardai.

"Tom, we can't play this one by the rules. He's the fucking Commissioner, for God's sake. How quickly do you think he's going to act? I'll tell you what they'll do—they'll open a file on the matter, and it will sit there, gathering dust, for years. We don't have any proof. I'm telling you, Tom, Cullen's a hothead. Wear a wire and provoke him. Then at least I have something tangible to hit him with, and maybe I'll get to go home."

Brannigan was very pleasantly surprised at the hearing they got from the Ombudsman. Tom had connections there, and it didn't take long to organise a meeting directly with the Ombudsman himself. He listened intently while Tom explained every detail to him emphasising the urgency of the matter. At this stage, Big O knew everything, and it was only a matter of time before the full story would leak out and get back to Cullen if it had not already done so. It was Tom who suggested they put a wire on their phones, and on Cullen's phone, and that he would meet with Cullen to try and push him into action.

"I have to get a judge to sign off on this," the Ombudsman explained as he left the room.

He had heard many rumours about the current Commissioner, particularly in relation to his past, and he personally despised the man. He was an arrogant bully. But this was the first time he had anything concrete on him.

And now, two days later, in a simultaneous operation involving the Head of the ATU, he had the pleasure of cuffing Commissioner Cullen and arresting him for perverting the course of justice.

Chapter 45

SHE SAT, WAITING patiently for him. It had been a very long time since she was inside a prison, and it was an experience that she hoped she'd never have to go through again. However, this prison was totally different. Everything was relaxed and low-key, and it seemed as if the prisoners could come and go as they please. So much for hard time, she shrugged.

"Hello," Shane stuttered when he saw her. He was surprised when the prison officer came into the library to inform him he had a visitor. Like most days, he could be found sitting there reading his books. He wasn't expecting anybody, but he was totally astounded when the officer told him her name. He felt physically sick.

"Hi, Shane," Mary Ryan forced a smile. "It's been a very long time."

"Over forty years."

"You look well." She wasn't lying. Just past his sixtieth birthday, he was now a very distinguished-looking handsome man.

"You too." He lied. He would have struggled to recognise the old woman now sitting opposite him. He remembered she was such a looker in her day. He quickly calculated that she must be the wrong side of eighty at this stage.

They both just looked at each other, neither of them knowing what to say. There was a time they were close. She had been like a surrogate mother to him. The memories came flooding back to him, like a tsunami in his head. Happy, carefree days, filled with laughter and sunshine. He had forgotten what happiness felt like. The last time he had experienced it was the night Mary Kate was attacked.

"Mrs. Ryan," he felt he had to break the silence.

"Shane, when in your life did you call me Mrs. Ryan? I remember the first day you swanned into our kitchen with Jamie, and I offered to make the two of you some sandwiches. *Sure that would be lovely, Mary,* you replied. Cheeky little imp, you were." She giggled. "Mary is still fine with me Shane."

"Thank you," he replied, but he couldn't bring himself to say her name. It just didn't feel right. It was too familiar and, Shane thought, disrespectful.

"Shane," she started, "I'm absolutely delighted that you finally managed to clear Jamie's name. It means everything to my family and me. I came here to thank you." Then she did something that took him totally by surprise. She reached out and gently rubbed his hand.

He didn't mean to recoil, but he did. He just couldn't handle what was happening.

"There's nothing to thank me for." His gaze was firmly fixed on a point on the table, refusing to make eye contact with her. He felt so utterly ashamed. It did not go unnoticed.

"Well, at least, the truth is out there now. And Cullen will get what's due to him. That's what you've always wanted—to find the truth, Shane. That's what we all wanted. Well, now the truth is out."

"Yes, but there's no salvation in the truth. What I did is unforgivable. It was savage and barbaric. You must really hate me." Again, he spoke to the table, not even attempting to raise his head.

"Were you aware I had a nervous breakdown?" she seemed to be changing the subject.

He slowly nodded.

"I actually like to call it my breakthrough." She smiled at him. "It taught me that hatred only destroys the spirit, it suffocates it to death. You know, I was so proud of you when you stood by him. It meant so much to me that Jamie wasn't facing it all alone. But then you cruelly extinguished his life. Yes, Shane, I won't lie to you. I did hate you once. In fact, I hated you for a long time." She spoke with such calmness and composure. Shane now had his elbows on the table, and his head in his hands.

"Shane…" she continued, "look at me, please."

He hesitated, and then slowly lifted his head until their eyes met.

"What you did was wrong, and I will never understand it. But that is in the past, and we can't change the past. That's not why I'm here. Tom Dylan came to see me yesterday, and he informed me of your decision. He asked me to come and talk to you."

"He shouldn't have done that. He had no right to. I'm sorry about that. I'll speak to him."

"No, Shane. I'm glad he did. I haven't been able to stop thinking about it. You know, whenever I'm puzzled or confused I often take solace in talking to Jamie. I know his spirit is always with me. And I was thinking what would Jamie want? Would he really want you to stay in prison for the rest of your life?"

"That was my sentence."

She ignored him and continued.

"Or, would he want you to put your life to some good? I'm aware that you thought that discovering the truth would set you free. It would bring you closure. But now you know you slaughtered an innocent man, your best friend. So, your solution is to continue punishing yourself, to stay locked up in prison for the rest of your life. Shane, listen to me. If Jamie were sitting here right now, what would he say to you?"

"I don't know," he whispered.

"Rubbish. You know very well what he would say. Anyway, I'm going to ask you to do two things for me, and we both agree that you owe me that at least." A hint of aggression had crept into her voice.

"If I can do them, I certainly will."

"There are no ifs. You'll do them for me. Agreed?"

"Yes."

"Firstly, end it. You could have been free over eighteen years ago when you first became eligible for release under license. You are not a threat to the State, and you've served your time. The Minister's view of your case is well documented. He cannot release you unless you apply for release, and he cannot force you to do that. Successive ministers have publicly stated that they would look favourably on your application. So the only thing keeping you in prison is you. For God's sake, they even looked at changing the law so that they could release you. You probably think it's the right thing to do, the honourable thing, but you're wrong, Shane. It's not. It's stupid and actually, selfish. There are other people you have to think of as well. What about your mother? She deserves to see her son a free man before she dies. What about my wishes? Most important of all—what would Jamie want? No good is coming from this. End this madness now."

Shane didn't move. He couldn't.

"Secondly, when you're free I want you to devote your life to the good of others. The media has always shown a remarkable fascination with you. You're hot property, and that will go through the roof when the full story comes out. According to Tom, that could be very shortly. That will make you a very famous man, a powerful person. The second thing you must do is to make that power count. Use your celebrity status to do some good. You will have massive earning power. Exploit it to its maximum. Use all your resources to promote good causes. That way, your life will

252

have real meaning and some good may come out of this. In some way, Mary Kate and Jamie won't have died in vain."

Shane looked at her and slowly shook his head.

"What I did was so wrong. I don't deserve another chance."

"I don't think it's as simple as that. You're a coward."

"Yes," he said. He didn't know where she was going with this, but he wasn't going to contradict her.

"You've been in prison for so long you're terrified to face the outside world. You must face your fears and overpower them. We will all help you."

He was about to speak but instead, started thinking about what she had just said. Maybe she had hit the nail on the head. Could he actually start again, leave this place and—

"Shane, I forgive you."

The words startled him. Nobody had ever said them to him, not that he ever expected to hear them. But to hear them from Jamie Ryan's mother! The last few months had been such an emotional drain, he genuinely felt he couldn't take much more.

"Shane," she pressed forward, "if I can forgive you, you must forgive yourself. Can you do that?"

He gently sobbed. He fought so hard to keep it in, but it was futile.

She stood up and went over to him.

"But first, Shane, I need to hear you say it. You must say it. That will set you free. It's only then that the healing will commence," she whispered into his ear.

He couldn't do it, he wanted to, but the words wouldn't come. He had wanted to say it from the moment he did it. He wanted to say it for over forty years.

"Say it, Shane. Please, Shane. I have to hear you say it," she implored him.

"I'm sorry. I'm so sorry."

She cradled him as they both wept.

Chapter 46

IT WAS MOST unlike him, and he knew it. The first tranche of money was in the bank, and he finally had his passport back in his hands. Today was the day Ned Brannigan would finally return home after his extended stay in Ireland. He greatly resented the fact that his stay was not by choice, but funnily enough, he had started to fall in love with Ireland. Who knows, maybe someday he would return. After all, it was his ancestral home!

Yet here he was, about to knock on her front door. He knew she was home alone—old habits die hard. Usually, he would just move on, nothing really mattered to him. Even though he had been married twice and was the father of two grown-up kids, Ned Brannigan didn't really connect with people. Sure, he could put on the pretence when he needed something, but in general, he was very happy in his own company. But Jamie Ryan meant something to him. He couldn't explain it. He just couldn't return home without letting her know.

Siobhan O'Donnell took a step back when she opened the door. She tensed up immediately.

"Hello, Mrs. O'Donnell. I'm sorry our last meeting ended so abruptly. I'd be grateful if you could just give me a few more minutes of your time." Brannigan turned on the charm, but he could see she was immune to it. She had seen his true colours.

"I'm not very comfortable talking to you. I want you to leave," she said, and she went to close the door. But she didn't slam it shut. She closed it slowly, and Brannigan noticed her hesitancy.

"Please," he begged. "There's something you need to know about Jamie Ryan," he shouted.

She stopped and re-opened the door slightly.

"What is it?" she asked nervously.

"May I come in?"

"No. You can tell me here." The door closed a bit more. He frightened her, and she was very conscious that nobody else was in the house. She was in two minds whether she should just go ahead, and close the door.

"Okay. That's fine. Please, there's nothing to be worried about." He picked up on her anxiety.

"I presume you've read the papers recently in connection with Commissioner Cullen?" he asked. Obviously, the arrest of the Garda Commissioner was a massive news story in Ireland but, for legal reasons, at the moment the details were very scant indeed. Little had been said except he had been arrested on a charge of perverting the course of justice.

"Yes. I've read about him."

"Well, in a way, it's all tied up with Jamie Ryan and Mary Kate Quinn. I thought you should know that Jamie Ryan was totally innocent. I'm not at liberty to tell you the whole truth now..." Big O had him tied up with one of his Confidentiality Agreements. "But it will all come out in time. I just wanted you to know."

"Thank you." She seemed to be on autopilot, and he wasn't sure if the words even registered with her.

"And, for reasons that will become apparent to you later, I firmly believe that Jamie Ryan had no intention whatsoever of harming you that night."

She nodded her head.

"That's all I came out to tell you. I thought you should know. Good day to you." Brannigan finished and turned on his heels.

He was halfway down the drive when she came running after him.

"Wait," she yelled.

He stopped and turned towards her.

"That night when I was leaving, you slipped something into my bag, didn't you?"

Brannigan hadn't forgotten about it and had contemplated on numerous occasions retrieving the envelope. But, with Cullen watching him like a hawk, it was always too risky. And then, when they solved the case without it, there was no need to get it back.

"Yes, I did." There was no point in lying.

"That was very kind of you. I never got a chance to thank you for the extra money. It was so generous. Twenty thousand euros made such a difference to our lives."

"Twenty thousand!" He couldn't even disguise his surprise. All he could do was laugh as he kissed her gently on the cheek.

Wasn't that something, Just plain old-fashioned money in the envelope—no big secret. Well, where else would you keep money except in a safe, he thought.

"And one last thing, Mr. Brannigan. I don't need any proof that Jamie didn't mean me any harm that night. I realised that years ago. It was just that bastard, Cullen."

SITTING IN THE back of the taxi going out to the airport, Ned Brannigan felt content.

"You ever hear of the Jamie Ryan case?" the taxi man asked.

Déjà vu.

"Yes, sure. Why?"

"Oh, it's just the murder took place in a small apartment block, just down that side street there."

Brannigan laughed. Obviously, a standard conversation piece for taximen around this area. But then it got Brannigan thinking.

What if, the first time he was leaving, the taxi man hadn't said anything? If he hadn't decided to stop?

And then the bizarre manner in which he had gained access to the apartment. Young Greg just letting him in, thinking he was the plumber.

Without any of these coincidences, the case would never have been solved.

And as they drove on past the café where Brannigan learned the final piece of the jigsaw that Cullen knew all along they had the wrong man. What a coincidence that he would meet Peter Molloy, who would tell him all about his father.

An unbelievable calmness suddenly descended on him. Ned Brannigan didn't believe in coincidences. Maybe there was something bigger at work here, something that guided him all along.

> *"This is what the Lord asks of you,*
> *Only this: that you act justly,*
> *That you love tenderly,*
> *And that you walk humbly with your God."*
> Micah 6:8

Acknowledgments

Finally getting to express how grateful I am to everyone who encouraged me and helped me to achieve my goal.

To my Mam, the greatest mother anybody could ever wish for. Without your positivity and encouragement, this book would never have been completed.

Also, to another one of my earlier readers, my aunt Imelda Bane. Thank you for taking the time to read the earlier drafts and for all your kind words.

To my brothers, Johnny, Tim, Michael, and Austin, and my sisters, Sinéad, Mary, Blánaid (and baby Aoife), a good old-fashioned Irish family! Thank you all for your thoughtful feedback and the speed in which you all got back to me with your comments. Love you all.

Also, to my extended family and the many friends and work colleagues—a big thank you. You are too numerous to mention. Sorry for plaguing you looking for feedback. I bet many of you wished you had never been given a copy of the manuscript:
"What stage are you at?"
"Are you finished yet?"
"What did you think?"
Oh, the writer's craving to be praised.

A particular mention to Kevin McCabe for all his IT assistance. Thanks, Kev.

On the editing side, there are two people I have to thank. The first person is Lar Dempsey, my old English teacher, who probably regretted sitting down beside me late one night at a school reunion. Lar is eighty something years young and spent a whole summer freely giving up his time going through the manuscript with me, line by line. Thank you, Lar, firstly, for making your English classes enjoyable all those years ago and secondly, for the sheer amount of time and excellent advice you gave me. What a man.

For the professional edit, format and proofreading, thank you to Rogena Mitchell-Jones (www.rogenamitchell.com). An absolute pleasure to deal with.

The original design for the book cover was done by my beautiful daughter Sarah, who came up with it and drew it in about five minutes. Thanks to Najla Qamber who brought it to life. (www.najlaqamberdesigns.com)

Thanks also to Janelle Harris, who also writes under the name Brooke Harris, for encouraging me and for giving me the heads up on self-publishing. Thanks, Janelle.

To John Murray and Liz Nugent—thanks for your kind testimonials.

Now, for the real hard part, how to thank my wife and kids?

Thank you Gráinne, my beautiful wife and best friend. Thank you for being firm with your comments and for not pandering to my needs. I know we had many a heated discussion, but I always appreciated and respected your opinion. You are my rock.

To my beautiful daughter Sarah. Thanks for your encouragement – "Just shut up and get it finished!" Seriously, thanks a million, and your carefully chosen few words were always insightful and valuable.

To my son Timmy, who supported and encouraged me all the way. I hope you never lose your caring nature.

Love you guys.

To my Dad, always loved and sadly missed. Never forgotten.

Finally, to you, the reader. Thank you for taking the time to read my book. I sincerely hope you enjoyed it.

www.brianacleary.com

About the Author

Brian Cleary lives in Dublin, Ireland with his wife, two kids, and two dogs. This is his debut novel.

About the Author